INFERNO

www.chellebliss.com

CHELLE BLISS
USA TODAY BESTSELLING AUTHOR

MENOFINKED.COM/HEATWAVE

1

STONE

"What a douchebag," Gigi mumbles under her breath as she walks up behind me at the countertop.

"Who?" I ask casually, but I don't give her response my full attention as I check my schedule for tomorrow.

My cousins, especially the females, think most people are douchebags. They have a high bar when it comes to behavior. I'm sure they've called me a douchebag more than once in my life, and honestly, I probably deserved it too.

She stabs at the keyboard with her thin fingers, clearly annoyed. "My client."

"What'd he do?"

Her fingers move faster as she shifts her weight to the other foot. "He talks to his girlfriend like she's a piece of trash."

I turn my head toward her, surprised she's over here

taking her frustration out on the keyboard and not his face. "And you didn't put him in his place or throw his ass out?"

Gigi sighs. "I try to hold my anger in check when it comes to customers. And he was fine until close to the end, or else I would've tossed him earlier. He's getting blacklisted, though. I'm not dealing with him ever again."

"Want me to cash him out?" I ask her, knowing most men, at least sane ones, won't hassle me. Anyone who picks on a woman is weak, but they're usually not dumb enough to start shit with me.

She shakes her head and finally gives the keyboard a break, turning her attention toward me. "I'll deal with him and drop the news about not coming back."

"I'll stay here, then. I'm not leaving you with him."

Gigi touches my arm and gives it a light, reassuring squeeze. "I can handle him."

I shake my head, refusing to leave her alone to deal with an asshole. "I got your back."

"What the fuck, Opal. You had one goddamn job," a man says loudly as he stomps into the front of the shop. "Only you could fuck it up."

A woman—Opal, I presume—has her head down, staring at her feet as she hurries up behind him. Her long brown hair hides her face. "I'm sorry... I didn't..."

"Save it." He lifts a hand, silencing her. "Useless bitch," he mutters.

My shoulders rise, and all the hairs on my body stand on end. My blood's pumping faster, and my heart has picked up with every clomp of his boots against the tile floor.

There are very few things that bother me in the world, and one of them is when men talk to women like they're trash. Men like him are the worst of the worst. No doubt he's not giving her the full wrath of his bullshit in front of us. This is probably his better behavior, which pisses me off more.

Gigi's eyes meet mine, and I know her skin's crawling without her having to say a word.

No one—and I mean *no one*—in our family talks to women like this. If we even get close, we better run because someone's going to beat our ass, and it's probably going to be a woman dishing out the punishment.

"I don't even know why I keep you around," the man seethes, not letting up or showing any grace.

"But I—" Opal starts to say, finally lifting her face up to his.

I suck in a breath, feeling like I've been punched in the gut at the sheer sight of her.

She's stunning.

Her eyes are the most haunting shade of blue against her tanned skin.

"Save it," he snaps.

Opal jerks, and I see a slight tremble in her body as she stands next to him. "Don't—"

He gives a look I can only describe as murderous. "Don't what?"

I've never given that look to anyone, not even an enemy.

Gigi stares at me, tipping her head in an *I told you so* motion. And I don't think the guy's a douchebag; I think he's an abusive asshole who doesn't deserve a creature as beautiful as Opal.

"Don't be mean to me, Jeff," she says in a timid voice that doesn't convey an ounce of authority.

Jeff "the douchebag" isn't fazed by her request. "Zip it. We'll deal with this at home."

That's my cue.

I'm not going to let her wait for her punishment when they're in private. I have only so much patience for bullshit, and he passed that moment two minutes ago. No one lays their hands on a woman, and no one talks to one like they're absolute trash. Not if I have anything to do with it.

But I'm at work.

A business my family owns.

I have to be careful, not laying my hands on him, even though I want to beat him to a bloody pulp until he's the one begging. Doing that will only open us up to lawsuits and shit we don't need to be dealing with for years to come.

I round the counter before Jeff has another chance to talk to Opal. "I think you should go," I tell him, stepping right into his personal space and towering over him.

He glares at me before his eyes dip down to my arms.

Yeah, sucker.

I'm built and bigger than you are.

I'll have no problem beating you without even breaking a sweat.

"Excuse me?"

"You can go now," I repeat, because he's clearly not getting my meaning. "Leave."

He reaches into his back pocket to fish out his wallet, but I lift my hand. "I mean right this fucking second."

"But I have to…"

It's my turn to lift my hand and shut him up. "No, you don't. We don't want your money or your business."

He laughs like I'm an idiot. "Whatever, man. I don't need this shit. It's a trash tattoo anyway."

Gigi growls, and I know she's holding herself back because the woman would love nothing more than to launch herself over the counter and strangle him.

He reaches for Opal and wraps his hand around her wrist, trying to tug her forward. "Let's go."

Opal doesn't move, digging her rubber heels into the floor. "No," she whispers.

His entire body goes rigid, and he slowly turns his face toward her. "I'm not asking."

I step toward Opal, not letting her leave with him under any circumstances. If I have to knock him out and dump him in the parking lot, I'll do it. I'll deal with the consequences of my actions later.

We've officially hit the fuck around and find out portion of the day for Jeff.

Opal's lip quivers, and her eyes become glassy. "I don't want to go with you," she tells him again.

I put myself between them, her arm brushing against my hip as he holds on to her like she's his personal property.

"You heard the woman. She's not leaving," I inform him, cracking my knuckles.

His dark green eyes narrow as his lip curls. "What are you going to do, meathead? Beat me up?" He laughs like the idea is lunacy, but I've beaten bigger men for far less than the way he's acting toward Opal.

"Yep," I snap. "And I'll enjoy it too." I move my gaze over his shoulder to Gigi, and I pray she can read my mind a little when I make the next statement. It'll be make-it or break-it without becoming a major incident. "I'll give you the first shot free and clear. If you can knock me off-balance, you can take Opal and go."

Opal gasps from behind me.

I have a good fifty pounds on him, and I've spent most of my life taking punches from guys bigger than he is. It doesn't hurt that my father was an MMA fighting champion and taught me how to take a punch.

"Deal?" I ask as I see Gigi coming around the desk from the other direction, reading my mind.

Jeff slides his gaze from me, around my side, to where Opal is standing. "She's not worth the hurt I'm going to give you," he says, clenching his hand into a tight fist.

I cross my arms over my chest, making it clear that I'm not going to hit him back. "You a pussy?"

His nostrils flare. "I'm not a pussy. But she's honestly not worth the hassle. You can deal with her lazy-ass, annoying behavior. I'm done with her. She's a lousy fuck anyway." He drops her hand and takes a step away. "She's good for nothing."

Opal sniffles behind me, and I can't bring myself to look at her. I've seen enough hurt on her face to last me a lifetime, and I've only known her for a few minutes.

I stalk forward, making him back up faster. "Out you go," I tell him, balling one hand into a fist.

"Hit me and I'll sue," he threatens, not surprising me at all.

Pussies always want to resort to a ridiculous threat because they know they can't win when it comes to strength.

He's the typical abuser.

Demean someone with words and even physically, but only because they're smaller and weaker.

He's a bully and deserves to feel the same type of pain, but now isn't the place or the time.

"Get the fuck out!" I yell, finally raising my voice and running out of patience.

He flinches.

I smirk, moving toward him so he doesn't waste any more of our time. "Now!"

He punches open the door, walking quickly to his shiny sports car that no doubt is his way of making up for all the other ways he's lacking.

I keep my gaze pinned on him, taking a few deep breaths to calm my breathing.

"It'll be okay," Gigi says softly behind me. "Don't cry."

I squeeze my eyes shut, hating that someone so beautiful and soft is shedding a tear for that waste of a human being.

"What am I supposed to do now?" Opal asks Gigi.

"I don't know, honey. Do you want a ride somewhere?" There's a pause and no response. "Any friends?" Again, a pause and no response. "There's a hotel nearby."

I turn around, soaking in the sight of Opal in one chair and Gigi in another. Gigi's stroking Opal's back as she leans over the chair, looking like she's about to be sick.

"I'll figure something out," Opal says.

"There are tons of hotels a little farther down the coast," Gigi tells her.

"I don't have any money for a hotel," Opal says softly. "My purse and phone are at Jeff's place. I'm not allowed to bring them with me when we're together."

It's not shocking that he isn't only abusive, but also controlling.

"I have a spare room," I say without much thought. "You can stay with me tonight and grab your purse tomorrow."

She lifts her head, and her blue eyes framed in red meet mine, looking wary. "I don't think…"

I want to say something, but I don't. She's been interrupted enough tonight.

"I don't know," she says. "You've already done so much."

"I could put her on my couch, cousin," Gigi says, still rubbing her back.

"You're family?" Opal asks, sitting a little straighter.

"Everyone here is. This is our family's shop."

Opal cracks the slightest smile as she wipes some tears away from her cheeks. "That's so sweet."

"My cousin over there may seem like a big ogre, but he's really kind, even if he's cocky as hell sometimes."

Opal straightens her back a little more and lifts her head a little higher. "I'll figure something out. I don't want to be a bother in anyone else's life."

"Darlin'," I say, taking a page out of Pike's playbook. "It's no bother. I got you into this situation, and it's the least I can do. Stay the night at my place, and you can grab your purse tomorrow."

"He's safe," Gigi assures her, moving her hand from Opal's back to touch her hand. "He won't try anything funny or else I'll have his balls in a vise, and I'm pretty sure he's attached to them."

I jerk my head back, playing along. "You wouldn't dare."

Gigi smirks. "If that isn't enough, I'll tell his mother, and no one makes that man shake as much as his mother. The woman is a saint, but the evil eye she gives is fierce."

Opal's smile grows a little larger. "He's scared of his mother?"

Gigi nods a few times. "Terrified."

"Gigi," I warn, hating that she's spilling my secret.

"He's like his dad, though. He's crazy protective of the

women in this family. He won't let anything happen to you. I wouldn't steer you wrong and send you from one bad situation to another."

Opal stares at me, her eyes flitting around my body. She's appraising me for safety.

Jeff was nothing special, and the man was no doubt more vicious in private than in public.

"Are you sure?" she asks me.

"Never more sure of anything in my life," I tell her, lying through my teeth. "And if it doesn't feel right when you're there, I'll take you wherever you want to go."

While I'm sure about the offer, I'm not sure that my life will ever be the same.

Something about the way Opal stares at me and the way my heart skips tells me life's about to change forever.

2

OPAL

"You seem nervous. Are you sure there's not somewhere you want me to drop you?" he asks as he drives, focusing on the road.

Fuck.

I'm an idiot.

How in the hell did I get myself into this kind of mess?

Jeff begged me to move to Florida with him, promising me all kinds of grand things, including him getting counseling.

I had a great-paying job in Chicago, but the warm weather of Florida was too hard to say no to.

"I'm not nervous," I lie, pulling my hands apart after I've fidgeted most of the ride. "You could drop me at a shelter if it's better for you."

"Is it better for you?"

I stare at his profile, taking in the handsome ruggedness of his features. "It's not like I'm in any position to be picky."

He turns his head, looking at me with eyes that disappear when the oncoming car passes. "You don't have anyone here?"

I sigh and sink into the seat. "I moved here a few weeks ago. I haven't had time to meet anybody yet. I know literally no one."

"That's awful."

"Yeah," I mutter.

It's also stupid. I've been on my own for years and knew better, but here I am.

Way to go, Opal.

When I was sixteen, my dad passed away, and a year later, my mother died too, leaving me in the foster system for a year before I was ejected into the world with no one and nothing. A few other foster kids became my friends and taught me the way to be street-smart and keep myself alive.

I thought I was doing a bang-up job of it until I met Jeff, and all my intelligence went right out the window. He sucked me in, made me feel like I finally had someone in my life I could depend on.

I knew he was an asshole, but when you don't have many options, an asshole sometimes seems better than being alone. I'd spent far too long by myself to want to go back to that life.

But after only a few minutes away from him, I feel my

body starting to relax, and my heart is no longer racing erratically for no reason at all.

My anxiety is dissipating. Anxiety he caused.

"Why don't you drop me off in the center of town? I can figure it out from there."

I figured it out when I was eighteen and homeless. What's the difference now?

It's a warmer climate, so it's not like I'm going to freeze to death. I've seen the homeless people on the sides of the roads here and begging for money at the intersections. They're surviving, and I have no doubt that I will too.

"Figure it out?" He repeats my words back to me but forms it like a question.

"Yeah," I mutter, nodding in the darkness. "Wouldn't you figure it out if you were in my circumstances?"

"Well..." He pauses, adjusting his large frame in the driver's seat of his truck as his fingers tighten around the steering wheel, "I guess I would, but it's different."

I turn my body so I'm facing him. "How?" I already know what he's going to say without his having to utter the words.

"I'm a man."

Ding. Ding. Ding.

There we go.

He's a man and somehow can take care of himself, whereas I cannot because of my breasts.

"I'm just as capable."

He grunts but doesn't look my way. "Darlin'," he says,

and I hate that my heart flutters at that word. "No offense, but…"

Anytime someone says no offense, they are about to offend the fuck out of you. And while there may be a smidge of truth to his words when it comes to strength, there are no other reasons I can't make it on my own, unlike him and his penis.

"I've been homeless before," I blurt out, wanting to prove a point and not caring about sharing more details with him than I do with many people in my life.

That gets his full attention. He turns his gaze toward me as we idle at a red light. "No shit. Really?" I can hear the astonishment in his voice.

"Yep. When I was eighteen and for about a year. And even with my tits and ass, I somehow survived. I think I could do it again."

"That's some crazy shit. At eighteen?"

"Yeah. It was a learning experience."

"I didn't mean anything by you being a woman."

"No?"

He shakes his head, easing off the brake when the light turns green. I take the opportunity to stare at him, memorizing the little details of his masculine face. "There're so many shady fuckers out there."

"Oh, I'm aware. I trusted no one until I met Jeff, and you know how well that turned out. But really, drop me off where there are other people, and I'll figure it out for the night."

"It's late."

"And?"

"It's too late to be dropped somewhere with no money or phone. Where would you go?"

I shrug even though he can't see me. "Everyone goes somewhere. Tomorrow, I'll get my purse and find a new place to live."

"That's not an answer."

"It is, but obviously not one you're willing to accept."

He shakes his head. "Nope. I don't accept it. I can't drop you off and drive away, going on with my night like nothing happened. What kind of person would do that?"

My foster parents and Jeff.

Jeff did it tonight without any thought for my safety, and my foster parents did that when I was still a kid. As soon as the checks stopped rolling in, I was pushed right out.

"Don't give it a second thought," I reassure him. "I promise to stay alive. Just forget about me."

He drives in silence without replying to my statement. As we approach a bar with a bright sign reading *Neon Cowboy,* he pulls in, parking close to the street but facing the front entrance.

I don't say anything as he cuts the engine and sits absolutely still for a few seconds.

I reach for the door, figuring he's already checked out and is just waiting for me to make my exit.

"Opal," he says softly before I have a chance to pull the handle.

I look at him, his face illuminated by the sign. "Yeah?" I ask as my stomach twists.

His emerald eyes meet mine, making the knot in my stomach vanish. "Stay for a night, and if you want me to drop you somewhere tomorrow, I will. Please," he begs. "I can't leave you here and go home, falling asleep like nothing happened. I won't be able to live with myself, and yes, my mother would kick my ass, but that's beside the point."

"Don't tell her."

He grimaces and shakes his head. "I'd be surprised if she doesn't already know. My cousin Gigi has a big mouth, and nothing stays secret in my family for long."

"Tell her I found a friend."

His eyes widen as he pulls his head back, pressing his body into the door. "I'm not lying to my mom, Opal. We may keep a secret or two, but we don't lie to one another."

That's oddly refreshing. I don't think I know many people who don't lie. We all have things we'd rather not confess to, even if they're small.

"You wouldn't exactly be lying. I'll make fast friends with someone," I tell him, trying to alleviate his anxiety about leaving me here.

He turns his gaze toward the bar and grabs the steering wheel with one hand, gripping the leather tightly. "I can't force you to stay. You've had enough of that shit in your life, but I'm pleading with you…begging for you to let me help you—at least for tonight."

"I don't know," I say, keeping my fingers wrapped around the door handle. "It's not fair."

"To whom?"

"You," I whisper.

He exhales loudly. "Do you snore?"

I shake my head. "Not that I know of."

"Do you fart in your sleep?"

I shrug and snort. "I don't know. I'm asleep. Do you?"

"Sometimes," he says honestly. "Then why wouldn't it be fair?"

I blink and stare at him, having nothing other than the obvious. "You have a life, and I'm interrupting it."

"I'm going home to eat some old pizza and go to sleep. Unless you plan to not sleep and play loud music all night, you wouldn't be interrupting my night at all."

There's a knock at his window, and we both jump. He swings his head around to look at the two people outside, waving wildly.

"Fuck," he hisses before rolling down his window. "Hey." His mood immediately changes from annoyed to jovial. "What are you two doing here?"

An older man with a long gray beard smiles at him before his gaze moves to me. "Was about to ask you the same thing, kid."

"Funny running into you here, honey. Who's the girl?" the older, shorter woman asks, clinging to the man next to her.

"This is Opal," my rescuer says.

I've already forgotten his name, which should be a

crime. I was so lost in the moment that I didn't take any time to file away that bit of information.

"Hi, Opal," the woman says with the kindest smile and eyes. "You kids coming in for a drink?"

"No. It's late. I need to sleep."

The older man laughs. "Late? Stone, man. You've gotten old in a heartbeat."

Stone fits him too. He's big and wide. He looks solid although I haven't touched him. He was big enough to send Jeff out the door without even taking a shot at him.

"Adulting isn't all it's cracked up to be."

"This is about the time you used to head out to the club, and now you're running home to get some shut-eye?" the man says to Stone.

"Come in for a beer," the lady insists. "Just one. You and your girlfriend."

"I don't know, Auntie."

Auntie? This guy has family everywhere, and if I didn't know better, I'd think we were being followed by them.

I have no family, and with that, I never had to worry about running into anyone at a bar late at night. But part of me thinks that's nice and somehow I'm missing out on something.

"I have to get Opal home," he says.

But now's my shot. He's done enough for me for the night—hell, for a lifetime. This may be my only chance to walk away and leave him free and clear of my bullshit.

"Come on. I'll buy you two a beer or whatever girlie

shit your generation drinks now," the man insists, ticking his head toward the bar.

I giggle at that. I like this guy. He's rough-looking. Someone I'd probably have turned the other way from if I saw him coming toward me, but I would've been wrong. He has a kindness to him that has a way of drawing you in.

"You want a beer?" Stone asks me, pleading with his eyes for me to say no.

"Sure."

Stone closes his eyes, knowing I killed his hopes of getting away from his aunt and uncle. I feel a little bad, but not entirely. Having a drink and making an older couple happy outweighs Stone's old pizza.

"Is the kitchen still open?" Stone asks.

"Sure as fuck is," the man replies.

"I'm starving," Stone says, scratching his stomach through his T-shirt. "Fine. We'll come for one drink."

The older woman's smile grows wider. "Fan-fucking-tastic. We never get you to ourselves, and with such a lovely lady too. This is a treat."

The couple backs away from the car, and Stone puts up his window, grumbling under his breath. "There's no hope of keeping this a secret now. Sorry, Opal."

"No need to apologize, Stone. We'll have a drink, and I'll have a plan by the time we're finished."

"If your plan isn't solid, I have that spare bedroom with your name on it."

"Okay."

"Just so you know," he says as he reaches for his

door handle, "Bear and Fran are nosy as hell. They're going to ask questions and a lot of them. I'll let you answer, and I'll follow your lead. Tell them what you want, or stay quiet if you want me to do the talking. They're the nicest people, but they always want to know everything."

"Got it." I smile, wrapping my fingers around my door handle.

"Ready for this?"

I nod and push open my door, stepping into the damp evening air that smells like salt and the ocean. It's something I notice every time I walk outside. After growing up in Chicago, surrounded by the smells of the city, I never want to get used to the cleanness of the air here.

His aunt and uncle walk in front of us, holding hands like a couple of kids.

It makes my heart ache a little.

I want something like that.

Stone sneaks a glance at me as we walk toward the bar.

I want to reach out and wrap my arm around his, but I stop myself, remembering this isn't a date.

He may have saved me, but I'm still nothing to him and he's a stranger to me.

The music smacks us in the face as soon as the doors open. The bar isn't well lit, and there are people everywhere.

It's an easy place to blend in and get lost.

It's perfect for tonight.

"There's a table!" his aunt Fran says, shouting over the

music and waving her hand in the direction of the only open table in the place.

She hustles on her heels, which are way too high for a woman of her age, keeping her balance like she was born with a pair of them on her feet.

Fran pushes the crowd apart with her head held high like she owns the room.

I'd be surprised if she was taller than five two, but she commands her surroundings with nothing more than her attitude and confidence.

I envy her for that.

She slides into an empty chair, and her husband sits down next to her, leaving the seats across from them open.

Stone holds out his arm, letting me sit first. I take the chair opposite his aunt and prepare myself to be barraged with questions. Thankfully, the music will make it damn near impossible for us to carry on much of a conversation.

Fran plucks the plastic-covered menus from between the napkin holder and ketchup bottle and hands them out to each of us.

The menu is typical bar food, but everything my eyes land on makes my stomach rumble. I snacked on a bag of chips before we went to the tattoo shop five hours earlier.

Stone leans over, bringing his mouth next to my ear. "Get whatever you want," he says loudly, the vibrations of his voice sending a wave of electricity down my spine. "I got you."

The song ends, and for a moment, my ears ring, making me dizzy.

"We're going to take a thirty-minute break," the lead singer says into the microphone as a few people whistle their appreciation.

Eek.

Silence is the last thing I want, and I'm sure Stone feels the same way.

"Excellent. We can talk now," Fran says, setting her menu flat on the table and staring across at Stone and me. "How long have you two been dating?"

A knot forms in my throat because, like him, I hate lying. The woman appears to be so damn nice, and the last thing I want to do is lie to her face.

"We're not dating, Auntie. We're only friends."

Her lips flatten. "Shame," she mumbles. "You two make a very beautiful couple."

"Idiot," the older man mutters as he looks around the room like he isn't talking to his nephew.

I reach over and touch Stone's arm. I need to make an escape.

I like these people too much, and I've only been with them a few minutes.

I also like Stone way too much. I need to break away now before it becomes even a little bit harder.

"Can you order me some fries? I need to use the ladies' room."

He studies my face a little too long for my liking, but I keep my expression as neutral as possible, praying he can't read my mind. "Sure," he replies as his eyes narrow for the briefest of seconds.

I give him a smile as I squeeze his arm. "Thank you." I turn to the older couple and say, "I'll be right back."

"Take your time, honey. We're not going anywhere," Fran says.

I feel awful that I'm about to ruin her night, but this may be my only chance to leave.

"Hurry back. He's not known for his conversational skills," Bear says to me, but he's ticking his chin at Stone. "You're also prettier."

"I'm pretty," Stone argues as I climb to my feet, but then he turns to me. "Want me to come with you?"

I stagger for a second and catch myself with his shoulder.

Damn.

His name is perfect.

He's solid.

Not an ounce of squish to him.

"No. I'll be fine, and I'm sure there's a line. There always is." I give him a smile before I walk away, not looking back but fully knowing Stone's eyes are on me.

Some girl is going to be very lucky to have a man like him, but that girl isn't me.

3

STONE

A strange feeling washes over me as Opal walks away from the table, disappearing into the crowd.

"Where're the bathrooms?" I ask Aunt Fran.

She points the opposite direction from the way Opal headed.

I'm immediately on my feet as my heart races uncontrollably. "Be right back," I tell them, and I don't wait for a response before I'm on the move.

I stalk into the crowd, looking for Opal's long brown hair. When I spot her, she's almost to the door to the parking lot, making no effort to head in the direction Fran pointed.

Shit.

She's not going to the bathroom.

She's running away.

For a split second, I think about letting her go. She's a

grown woman and not my problem, but there's a part of me that stops that train of thought in its tracks.

She needs help but isn't willing to ask for it.

I get it. I really do.

I never like to ask for help or appear weak in any way, but everybody needs help at some point in their life.

When she opens the door and disappears into the parking lot, I pick up my pace before I lose her forever. I push people out of my way, not caring about being cussed out for being a prick.

I smack the door with my palms, forcing it open. Opal's heading toward the street. "Opal," I call out as I walk faster, almost running.

She stops walking but doesn't turn around. "I'll be fine," she replies, staring straight ahead. "You can go back inside. I'm not your problem."

That's a shitty way to think. Why would she view herself as a problem to anyone? "Wait." I stalk up behind her, reaching for my wallet.

She may not want to stay with me, but I can at least give her some money, so she's not left without a penny in her pocket.

It's the bare minimum I can do for a stranger, especially since I have so much.

I grab two crisp one-hundred-dollar bills from my wallet and fold them in half. "Take this," I say to her, holding out the money as I stand behind her.

She drops her head, staring at the cash next to her arm. "I can't take it."

I push the bills forward farther. "Take it. You need it more than I do. You need at least some cash in your pocket if you're going to leave."

"You've done enough, Stone."

I wince, feeling like that isn't a compliment because she wouldn't be on the street if I hadn't opened my mouth. She'd be at home with a guy who treats her like shit. "I haven't done enough, Opal. If you won't let me give you a place to crash, take the money."

Her eyes haven't left my hand holding the cash.

"At least get yourself a room for the night."

Her shoulders slump forward. "Fuck." She peers up, looking over her shoulder, meeting my eyes. "Why are you helping me?"

I shrug. "Why not?"

"It's not normal."

"I'm not normal, but normal is boring. I'm also not always the good guy, Opal. I have my own issues, but I've been blessed with a good family, a great business, and everything I could ever want or need. Just take the money. Please."

Fuck. It's never been so hard to get someone to take money from my own hands without any expectation of being paid back. Especially when that person doesn't have two pennies to rub together.

She exhales as her shoulders slump forward a little farther. "I don't…"

I stay silent. My hand is still out, money stuck between two fingers, waiting for her to take the cash.

"I don't feel right taking your money."

A wave of nausea washes over me. She's going to be alone and penniless. "Please. I won't be able to sleep tonight if you don't."

"You two kids coming back?" Fran says from behind us. "The server's waiting for us to order."

"Shit," Opal whispers.

Fran followed us, but it's not surprising. Not much gets by her, and she makes sure she knows everything that's going on. I swear she must've worked in intelligence when she was younger because she's like a relentless detective.

"Come back in and eat, and then you can disappear," I plead with her.

"Fine," she says, turning slowly to face me and my aunt Fran.

"Be right there, Auntie," I call out without looking back.

"Don't take too long," Fran replies before the music gets louder and then dull again.

Opal studies my face. "You people are too nice."

I crack a smile, knowing we can be a total pain in the ass too. But for once, I am happy about my aunt's nosiness. Without her walking out here, making Opal feel an ounce of guilt, she would've walked away with nothing.

"That's one way to describe us."

Opal moves slowly toward the Neon Cowboy, and I walk at her side, taking each step as she does. "Can I ask you something?"

"Maybe."

"Why were you homeless at eighteen?" I glance at her after I ask the question, but she doesn't seem fazed or bothered by my prying.

Her gaze is fixed on the doorway as she walks. "My foster parents turned me out when I legally became an adult. When the money stops coming in, they want to make room for someone new who will bring cash into the house."

An inexplicable anger comes over me at her admission. Who could do that to someone so young and vulnerable? "Is that how it is for everyone? Foster parents, I mean."

She shakes her head. "There are a lot of great foster families. But lucky me, I didn't get one of those. I wasn't there for long, so it wasn't like I was sad to go."

I can't imagine turning eighteen and being turned out onto the streets with no one and nothing.

"How did you end up in foster care?" I ask her, but then I feel like an asshole for prying into something that's none of my business. "You don't have to tell me."

Opal stops outside the entrance and turns to me, crossing her arms over her chest. "My parents died, and after that, I entered the system until I turned eighteen."

"I'm sorry," I say genuinely. "I can't even imagine."

"I'd never want you to," she whispers before reaching for the door.

I grab the handle, opening the door for her, letting her walk inside first. I follow her back to the table, taking in her lean frame and long hair. She almost glides across the floor to where Bear and Fran are waiting.

"Sorry about that," I say to them as I sit back down. "We needed to talk."

"No problem," Fran says, but she's staring at us like she knows there's something we're not saying.

The waitress arrives and we order, but before she walks away, Bear makes sure she knows he wants the check for all of us. My hunger is dulled by the thoughts of Opal's childhood and life struggles, but somehow, I still order a cheeseburger. She sticks to her original order, getting a side of fries and nothing else.

"Where ya from, Opal?" Aunt Fran asks, resting her chin in the meaty part of her palm she has propped up. "I hear some Midwest in you."

"Chicago."

Aunt Fran sits up a little straighter, suddenly more excited than usual. "No shit. Me too."

"Really?" Opal asks.

"Our entire family is from there," I tell Opal, thinking that's a strange coincidence.

"But I lived there for most of my life, while the other side—" Fran waves her hand at me "—left a long time ago."

"You're from Chicago too?" Opal asks me.

"My grandfather, Fran's brother, grew up there but moved to Florida over fifty years ago. But we do still have family there."

"What part are you from?" Fran asks Opal, glancing up when the waitress sets four beers on the table.

"The Loop."

"North or South?"

I stare at them because they may as well be speaking a different language. I have no idea what the Loop is or what it means to be from the north or south of it.

"South."

Fran gasps, slapping the table hard enough that our beers jiggle. "No shit. Me too. Where exactly?"

Opal doesn't answer for a moment as she wraps her small hand around the base of the beer bottle. The place isn't fancy enough for glasses. "Fifteenth and State near Canal."

Fran whistles. "Swanky."

Opal laughs. "I don't know if I'd call it swanky."

"Swankier than the Neon Cowboy."

Opal glances around, soaking in the redneck biker vibe that this place has in spades. "Yeah, I guess that much is true."

"Your parents still there?"

My body goes rigid and my stomach sinks. I hate this for Opal. How many times does she have to go over the same story, reliving the grief of her parents' deaths?

"No," Opal says, lifting the beer toward her mouth. "They passed ten years ago."

Fran's eyes widen. "Both of them?"

Opal nods as she takes a sip of her beer.

"Fuck. That sucks, kid. I'm so sorry," Fran says, trying to hide her frown behind her bottle.

"Shitty hand," Bear mutters before chugging down half of his beer in what seems like two seconds.

"It was a long time ago," Opal says, as if somehow the amount of time that's passed makes it easier to swallow the cold, hard truth of her past.

"You have family still there, at least? Go back often?"

Opal shakes her head again. "No. No one else is there."

"Ever think about going back? I do." Fran turns to look at Bear, who has an eyebrow raised.

"Like hell you are, woman. Your ass is staying here where it's warm and you can wear those sexy-as-fuck hot pants with your ass hanging out the bottom."

I almost spit out my beer. The image of my aunt Fran's ass sticking out of her pants as she walks has my stomach turning like I ate something rotten. It's not that she isn't beautiful. I'm just not at the age that old-lady bottom is something I want to see.

"Shut up." Fran smacks Bear in the arm as he takes another swig of his beer. "Don't talk that way in front of the children."

I turn my head, looking at Opal's smiling face. She's enjoying herself, liking the insanity that is Fran and Bear. It's hard to be anything but happy when they're around because they're laid-back with a dash of crazy.

"It's okay. You two are my life goal," Opal says.

"Aw," Fran gushes with a grin. "If you can nail that one down, I think you've got a good shot."

Opal's wide eyes swing to me.

"We're not dating," I tell Fran again.

"Not yet, but you will." She winks at me.

"No, we really aren't. We barely know each other,"

Opal adds, opening the floodgates to Fran asking even more questions.

"When did you meet?"

Here we go. The Franish Inquisition has started, and there's no stopping the train once it's rolling.

"Tonight," Opal answers.

Bear almost chokes on his drink, but somehow he recovers quickly. "You move fast, kid. I like your style." He says those words to me.

I give him a fake, uncomfortable smile as I turn the beer bottle in my hands, trying to make myself busy. I don't know what Opal wants to divulge to them, and I'm going to let her steer the conversation, so I don't insert my foot in my mouth.

"Wow," Fran mutters. "I can't believe that."

"It's true," I say, backing up Opal.

"Did we interrupt…" Fran waggles her eyebrows. "You know…?"

"Oh God, no," Opal says immediately, waving her hand over the table. A little too fast, really. As if the idea of her sleeping with me is somehow ridiculous. "He was giving me a ride."

"I bet he was." Fran grins.

Opal blushes, and I know I have to step in to stop the train from going completely off the rails.

"I was taking her home."

"Hers or yours?" Bear asks this time, waggling his eyebrows.

"Stop. It isn't like that. Opal's friend left her at the

shop, and I was giving her a ride so she wouldn't have to call a taxi."

There's instantly a scowl on Bear's face. "They left you?"

Opal's smile is tight. "Yep."

"That's shitty." Fran reaches across the table, setting her hand on Opal's. "He isn't worth it, babe. Any man who would leave you behind without a second thought isn't worth an ounce of your time or energy."

"Who said it was a man?" I ask.

"No woman is going to leave her friend behind in a tattoo shop, Stone. It goes against the sisterhood code."

I laugh. "That's ridiculous."

"Am I right?" Fran asks Opal. "Your friend is a he?"

Opal nods. "He's in the past now."

"Where he needs to stay gone and buried." Fran pats Opal's hand before pulling her arm back. "Stone will get you where you need to go. He's a good kid. A little wacky sometimes and loves the ladies a little too much, but he's a good egg."

I rub my forehead, hating that everyone thinks I'm a womanizer. I mean, they're not wrong. But why do they feel the need to tell everyone, including the pretty woman at my side? "I don't love the ladies too much, Auntie, and I'm not wacky."

"You're a player," Bear says with a grin. "And if I were your age, I would be too."

"I'm pretty damn sure you were worse than him at that age," Fran tells him.

"You only live once," Bear says as he slides his arm around the top of her chair, resting a hand on her shoulder. "But I'm a one-woman man now."

"If you want to stay alive," she mutters.

"You two are funny and cute," Opal tells them.

"We have our moments," Bear says, leaning over to give Fran a kiss on the cheek.

"Ah. The food's here," Fran says, breaking the moment of sweetness between her and Bear.

I let my body relax, knowing we'll be too busy eating to continue the same line of questioning. As soon as we're done, I'm taking Opal and we're leaving.

We're leaving. There's no way in hell I'm letting her out on the streets to fend for herself. I have too much in life, while she has nothing.

It's about damn time Opal knows kindness, and I am going to do my best to show her a little until she figures out her next move.

4

OPAL

"Do you want to get your purse tonight?" Stone asks me before we get up from the table.

I glance out of the corner of my eye, noticing Bear and Fran listening and watching us. "No. It's okay. I don't need it right now."

"Wait," Bear says, leaning forward. "You don't have your purse?"

"No," Stone answers him, staring at me when he does. "It's at his place."

Bear pushes aside his empty beer bottle. "The prick left you and knew you had no way to pay for anything or get anywhere?"

"Yep," Stone replies. "It's my fault, though."

I hate that he's taking the blame. I'm the one who's at fault for being with and staying with a guy who treated me like shit. I should've walked away a long time ago. "There's no one to blame except me."

Stone reaches out, placing his hand on mine as it rests on my knee. "The only one who did anything wrong here is Jeff."

"I know." I force a smile, trying not to argue with him.

"This guy ever hit you?" Bear asks, and I don't even mind the question. He's a charming older man, and although his exterior looks tough, he's been nothing but a sweetheart. And I have no doubt he loves his wife and cherishes the ground she walks on.

"No. He never hit me." But he had laid his hands on me a time or two. He got a kick out of grabbing my arms and restraining me when he saw fit in order to remind me that I was weaker than him.

"Maybe not yet, but it was coming," Fran adds. "Mark my words."

Based on the look on her face, she's had similar experiences to mine with men.

"Let's get the check and head over to his place to grab your purse. There's power in numbers, and that shit ain't going to stand. He doesn't get to keep your stuff," Bear says.

My stomach turns at the thought of a confrontation with Jeff. But I also know I can't do it alone.

"This isn't your problem," Stone tells Bear.

"It's not yours either," I remind Stone.

This is entirely my problem.

Bear runs his fingers across his beard, smirking. "I've been needing some action. I'd be delighted to go there with you and have your back. If I get to throw a punch or two, that's a bonus."

"Do you think that's a good idea at your age?" I can tell by the way Stone looks at Bear he's being sincere. His face is soft, and there isn't an ounce of enjoyment in his words. "If you get hurt…"

"Stone, kid, I could kick your ass with one hand tied behind my back. I may be *older*, but I'm sure as hell not old."

I smile as I stare at Stone's profile. I don't know why Bear's strong confidence and Stone's horrified concern make me happy. I've never been around a group of people that is so loving and spicy at the same time.

"Trust me, Uncle, you'd need two hands to even make me flinch."

Bear barks out a laugh. "Such a shithead. We doing this or what? Opal needs her purse, and my fist is itching to meet an asshole."

"Um," Stone mutters and glances at me. "That's up to Opal. It's her life, old man."

My eyes widen because I don't know what I want to do. I need my things, but I don't want to face Jeff tonight. I feel drained and uncertain about what's to come. On top of that, if one of them gets hurt because of my personal issues, I'd never forgive myself.

"I don't think we should go there tonight. He'll be at work tomorrow, and I can go then," I tell Stone and turn my gaze to Bear. "I appreciate your willingness to help, but I need to do this myself."

Bear shakes his head. "That doesn't work for me."

"It doesn't work for you?" I repeat his statement back in the form of a question.

He sinks his fingertip into his bushy salt-and-pepper beard as his eyes harden. "The last thing you need to do is go there alone. Either you take us, or you go in armed with some sort of weapon."

I jerk my head back, shocked. "A weapon?"

"A baseball bat, a gun, a Taser," Bear explains further like I don't know what a weapon is.

"For real?" I ask in disbelief.

"Fuck that," Stone snaps. "We're going with you. A weapon can easily be taken and used against you. It won't be as safe."

None of this seems safe—either for me or them. I have no doubt they could take Jeff, but at what cost to themselves? If one of them gets hurt…

"We won't get hurt. It'll be a quick job. Get in and get out, but we'll have your back," Bear says to me.

"It's late." I state the obvious.

Bear nods slowly. "That's perfect. Hopefully he'll be asleep, and his reaction time will be slow. It may help him be calmer too."

The man is never calm. I've been living in a heightened state for years, but I hadn't realized how stressed I was until the last few hours. The amount of relaxation I feel around the three people at this table is surprising.

"You want your things?" Stone asks with his head tilted and one hand on his chest. "We'll make it happen."

"I only want my purse and phone. Nothing else."

"Then let's do this shit," Stone says, repeating Bear's earlier words.

"Oh boy," Fran mutters, but she doesn't look pissed or worried. "This could be an interesting night."

Bear leans over to his wife, brushing a kiss against her lips. "It'll be fine, baby."

"You're sexy when you're protective," she whispers as she stares into his eyes.

"They're gross," Stone mutters, staring at them with a wince.

"They're great." I smile, watching the big, burly guy being sugary-sweet with his woman. They give me hope that love is real and that there are men out there who treat women well. "They're straight life goals."

"You ready to get out of here?" Stone asks.

I nod, but I don't feel great about any of this.

"Ready, old man?"

Bear releases his grip on Fran and gives Stone a chin lift. "Let's do this. I'll follow on my bike."

"Do I get to kick some ass?" Fran asks, looking almost giddy with anticipation.

"No," Bear tells her in a flat tone. "You're going to watch the bike."

"Sounds wonderful," she mutters, rolling her eyes. "They get to have all the fun. It's not fair."

"How far away is his place?" Stone asks me.

"Near the shop, down by the ice cream place."

"By the canals?" he asks.

I nod. "The place that looks like an old motel that's been converted to apartments."

"You know where, Bear?"

Bear gives Stone a nod. "I'll be right behind you."

Stone reaches out his arm and offers me his hand. "Let's get your things, baby, and get you on to something better."

I slide my hand in his, hoping what's left of my life after Jeff is better. But so far, life has sent me from one shitty situation to the next…present company excluded.

"I don't know how to thank you," I say.

"Just live a happy life without an asshole," Bear says, making it sound so simple.

"I'd do anything to see a smile on that face," Stone says, reaching up with his other hand to touch my cheek with a featherlight touch. "It's far too pretty to look so sad."

My face heats as his words wash over me. "I'm happy."

Happier than I've been in a while. I'm surrounded by three wonderful people and free from Jeff having an opinion about all the ways I've messed something up.

Fifteen minutes later, after a quiet car ride, we're standing outside what used to be my apartment.

Stone's holding my shoulders in his big hands as he explains the plan. "I'll knock, and you stay behind me until it's safe for you to get your stuff. Got it?"

I nod, trying to ignore the nausea that's rolling inside me in waves. I can do this. I wouldn't be able to do it without Bear and Stone, but it's still hard. Jeff's going to be upset and do his best to place the blame on me, making me out to be the bad guy.

Fran moves to my side, looking fiercely protective. "I'll watch her. You two do your thing."

Stone gives Fran a small nod of approval before turning his attention back toward me. "Get in, grab your purse and phone, and get out. Let's make this as quick and clean as possible."

"That's the plan," I assure him, hoping he doesn't notice the slight tremble in my body.

Stone turns away, and I resist the urge to call the entire thing off.

"It'll be fine," Fran whispers to me like she's reading my mind. "The guys are tough."

I don't say anything back to her. I'm too busy watching Stone as he knocks on the door and trying to push down the fear crawling up my throat.

Bear moves around me to have Stone's back.

I'm barely breathing as the light inside turns on. There's yelling, but that's not a surprise when it comes to Jeff. A normal tone of voice isn't his strong suit.

"What the fuck…" Jeff says as the door swings open. He's wearing nothing except a pair of boxers.

"Who's that?" a girl in a T-shirt asks, walking up behind Jeff with bare legs.

Well, he didn't waste any time.

He lifts a hand to silence her. "Jolene, go back to the bedroom."

"It's Joanne," she corrects him, not even looking mad that he called her the wrong name.

"Whatever. Go back there. This has nothing to do with you," he tells her, but he's looking straight at me.

And if looks could kill, I'd be fucking dead and buried. There's not an ounce of love or caring in his eyes, but that's not surprising with the way he treated me and how quickly he found another woman to warm his bed.

"Give us her purse and phone, and we'll go," Stone tells Jeff, calmer than I ever thought possible.

"This bitch has you out here handling her business."

Stone takes a step forward. "Watch it."

"Fuck you, man. And her. She's trash. If you're smart, you'll toss her out on the side of the road and wipe any memory of her from your mind."

Stone takes another step forward, leaving very little space between himself and Jeff. "Purse. Phone."

"Fuck this, kid," Bear says, pushing Stone to the side and going toe-to-toe with Jeff. "My nephew is nicer than me, but I have no problem knocking your ass out and taking her shit. Do you want to be blacked out or fucking in the next ten minutes?"

Jeff looks Bear up and down. "You going to knock me out, old man?" he laughs. "That's ripe."

Oh boy. He didn't call him old man in the nice way Stone did earlier. Jeff was calling into question Bear's manhood, and I think he is about to find out that age is only a number.

"You made the choice," Bear says, rearing his arm back and letting it rip.

The sound of Jeff's face being clocked by Bear's fist is something I'll never forget. The crunch of bone, the splattering of blood. *Yuck.*

But I can't stop staring at Jeff's head as it snaps back and then forward before he staggers, trying to find his footing. His hands move to his face, catching the blood that's streaming out of his nose like a faucet has been turned on.

"What the fuck," Jeff mumbles against his palm.

"I'm not old, you little-dick asshat. Purse and phone," Bear demands, not giving Jeff time to recover before making it clear what he wants for the second time.

"Fuck you," Jeff bites out, cupping the blood as it pours out of his left nostril.

I've never been hit that hard and I can't imagine what it feels like, but it has to be painful. I'd be seeing stars, unable to keep my balance. But somehow, Jeff's still standing.

"I take that as a no," Bear says, rearing back his other hand and clocking Jeff so hard in the side of his jaw that he staggers to the other side, crashing into the doorframe.

Jeff's body falls backward and flattens on the ceramic tile floor. Blood is still pouring from his nose out of both nostrils, but it's sliding down his face and pooling on the off-white flooring beneath his head.

"Is he okay?" I ask, gawking at Jeff's motionless body,

hoping he isn't dead. Not because I care about him, but because I don't want Bear to go to jail.

Bear peers down, staring at Jeff for a few seconds before he answers. "He's alive. He's only knocked out. Blood's still moving."

"Blood's still moving?" I ask, gawking at the blood as my stomach turns.

"Blood stops flowing when you're dead. He's alive, babe. Pricks like him don't deserve to be, but I'm too old for hard prison time again."

My eyes move from Jeff to Bear. Again? Bear said again. The man's been to prison? He's not what I think of when I picture a hardened criminal. He's sweet as pie.

"Go," Stone demands, touching my arm to get my attention. "We don't have much time." He glances around, looking at the windows of the neighbors. "Cops may be on the way already."

"Shit," I mumble, stepping over Jeff. "I'll be quick."

"You fuckers are going to jail," Joanne says. "Breaking and entering, along with theft. That's a heavy sentence too."

I ignore her as I move things around in the living room, finding my purse and phone hidden behind a couch cushion.

"I hope you like orange," she adds with one shoulder lower than the other and her arms crossed over her chest.

I spin around, glaring at the woman standing in what was my living room less than six hours ago. "Listen, bitch. This was my house, and that was my man. He's trash. He's abusive. But from what I'm getting, you're not a gentle little thing either. He's your problem now, not mine. But if I were you, I'd get dressed and run. Get as far away from that asshole as you can before you're standing in my shoes, being harassed by a woman who's eating your sloppy seconds." I place my slingback purse over my shoulder and stash my phone in my back pocket.

"Lying bitch. He told me about you," she seethes, clearly thinking I'm making shit up.

"Whatever." I throw up my hands, done with the bullshit. "He's your problem now. You two deserve each other." I stalk away from her, moving toward Bear, Stone, and Fran.

They're smiling, looking proud of me, which is such a foreign thing for me to see. No one has been proud of me since my parents died.

"Come on," Stone says, holding out a hand for me.

I grab on to him, using his steadiness as I step over Jeff. I don't look down. He's nothing to me anymore. He's part of my past. A bad memory. But one thing is for sure, he'll never be part of my future.

"Good job," Bear says to me, looking impressed.

"You okay?" Stone asks as I almost topple forward straight into him.

"I'm good," I tell him, which is kind of true—if I ignore the way my body's shaking.

"Stay with me tonight."

I gaze up at Stone, knowing I'd be safe. Although my judgment has been off in the past, this man has done nothing but be kind and caring to me since he put himself between Jeff and me. "Okay," I whisper.

Stone's smile wipes away any ounce of fear and doubt left inside me.

I have no idea what the future is going to hold, but I know it isn't going to be filled with fear. I'll never allow it again. And for the night, I'll have Stone to make sure I'm safe.

"Let's roll before the cops come," Bear says when we don't move fast enough.

We leave Jeff lying in the doorway, bleeding and motionless. He wouldn't give me a second look, and I do him the same courtesy.

"Thank you," I say to Stone as we rush to his truck.

"Anytime, Opal. I would've done more to keep you safe and make you happy."

I smile as I climb into the passenger seat of his truck, wondering what his idea of more is. He's already done too much.

"You deserve the world," he says as he closes the door.

Who is this man, and how did I get lucky enough to have him drop into my life, becoming my rescuer?

I've never been told I deserve anything, but the way Stone looks at me, I want to believe it's true.

Whatever happens from here on out, I'm going to try to lead a life worthy of their help, especially Stone's.

5

STONE

I tiptoe into the kitchen, needing coffee. My eyes are barely open as I push start, standing in front of the machine until I hear the familiar bubbling. I stretch, getting all the sleep out of my system along with the stiffness from being still for too long.

"Hey," a soft voice says from behind me, making me jump.

Opal. I'd forgotten she was here, which seems impossible after everything that happened last night.

"Mornin'," I reply, placing my palms on the countertop but not turning around.

My already granitelike morning wood gets a little bit harder with the sound of her voice and the remnants of her perfume in the room.

I wait a few seconds, thinking about all types of horrible shit, trying to make it go away.

The chair scrapes against the floor before she sits down. "Do you have enough for two cups?"

"Yep. I'm making an entire pot." I glance down, hoping my cock isn't on full display.

"Thank God," she says in this breathy tone that once again does nothing but aggravate my dick.

I grab two mugs out of the cupboard above the coffeemaker before sliding over to the fridge to get some cream. "You take sugar?"

"The sweeter, the better."

"Gotcha," I mutter, annoyed with myself and my dick.

He's always been a complication, getting me in more trouble than I want to admit. From an early age, he's given me nothing but problems. He has his useful moments, but there are occasions when he's begging for attention at the wrong time.

This is one of them.

"We forgot your car last night," I say to her, hoping to talk about something…anything to make him not so interested.

"It's at the shop. I'll call the dealership and see if they can pick me up so I can get it. Then I can get out of your hair. I appreciate everything you and Bear did for me last night, but I know when my time is up. And my time is up. You've done more than enough, and I don't know how I'm ever going to repay you."

I wonder what it's like to go through life feeling like a bother to everyone around you. Opal has a hard time accepting help, which I imagine made her ripe for the picking for Jeff. A man like him wants a woman who doesn't feel she's worthy of anything. It's how he was able to get and maintain power over her for as long as he did.

I keep my back to her, but this is something that should be said face-to-face. I try to stay busy so I don't seem rude, grabbing the sugar and spoons to prep our coffee. "I'll take you to get it. I don't have to be at work until four this afternoon. And we didn't do much, Opal. It's nothing I wouldn't do for any one of my friends or family."

"That must be nice," she whispers. "I can't imagine what that's like."

Finally, the pot is half full, and I'm unable to resist the urge to pour the first two cups. It'll be stronger than normal, but on a morning like this, it's needed. "I can't imagine not having people, but you've got people now, Opal."

"I do?"

I carry the mugs in one hand, looping my index finger through the two handles, and try to avoid spilling them as I hold the sugar and cream in my other hand. "You have us," I tell her as I set her mug on the table in front of her.

She stays silent, staring at me without giving any attention to the coffee.

I slide into the seat next to her, my normal spot where I drink my coffee every morning and check out what's happening in the world on my phone. "If you want us, I mean. No one should be alone."

"Why?"

"Why?" I repeat her question back to her, confused.

"Yeah," she says with a slight nod as she grabs on to her hair with her fingers, pulling at the ends. "Why do you want me?"

Fuck. That's a loaded question.

I don't want her to be alone, but if I'm honest, I'd love for Opal to be more than a friend. I'm not talking wife, but a girlfriend isn't entirely out of the realm of possibility. She's beautiful with her long hair, curvy figure, and an ass that is more than a handful.

"You can never have too many friends, and right now, it sounds like I'm your only one, if you don't count Bear and Fran."

She smiles at me for a moment before she reaches for the sugar and spoon I'd set down next to her coffee mug. "You guys are way too kind."

"I think we're normal. Maybe you've spent most of your life being surrounded by assholes."

She laughs quietly. "That's no lie."

"What are you going to do now?" I ask her, genuinely curious, but also concerned.

"Drink my coffee." She smirks against the rim of her mug.

I take a minute, studying her face as she takes a sip of her coffee and closes her eyes. Her skin is flawless even without makeup. Her dark brown eyebrows are perfectly groomed and arched to a point. Her lips are full and look as soft as silk. I can't help but stare at her mouth as she licks the remnants of coffee from her lips.

"And after that?" I ask, trying to talk about something so I can get my mind off her mouth and the way her tongue moves.

Opal shrugs. "I'll rent a hotel room for a few days until I find an apartment."

"You can stay here," I blurt out, clearly not fully awake or thinking straight.

Why did I say that? I haven't lived with anyone since I moved out of my parents' place. I never even have the women I'm sleeping with stay at my house.

"Until you find a place," I add, not wanting her to think I want her to stay here forever.

"A hotel is okay. You've done enough."

I raise an eyebrow. "Do you always have this much trouble taking help from people?"

Opal holds her coffee mug in two hands as she leans back in her chair and stares at me. "I guess so."

"But you took Jeff's help." It's a low blow, but I said it. I know as soon as the words leave my mouth that I shouldn't have mentioned his name. Now, I'll have to backpedal and hope to God she doesn't walk out the door immediately.

"Not at first," she says without an ounce of anger or agitation in her voice. "We dated casually for a long time. I didn't live with him until we moved here a few months ago. I wouldn't say he even helped me after that. I've always had my own money and learned not to rely on people."

"I misspoke. I'm sorry."

I'm an asshole. I don't know why I thought maybe she leaned on him, letting him control all aspects of her life.

"It's okay."

"No, it's not."

She takes another sip and closes her eyes again, savoring the taste. "I don't know what kind of coffee this is, but it's the best I've ever had."

"It's the chicory. It's smooth and strong, right?"

"It's like a little sip of heaven." She sets down her coffee, pulling her knee up against her body.

I glance down, catching a glimpse of her glitter-covered toenails. They're cute. Not what I was expecting or usually like, but somehow, they work.

"Anyway, in the beginning, Jeff was nice, but then he changed."

"Why didn't you leave?"

"Have you ever been alone? Like, really alone?"

I sit there, thinking about the question. I've never been alone. Not a moment in my life. If I wasn't with my parents, I was with my cousins or grandparents. Sometimes I wished I had some alone time, but now she's making me question everything.

"No. I haven't. Not a moment."

"See?" She waves her hand toward me. "You're lucky. I was so alone, and I'm not talking bored alone. I'm talking about why I was willing to put up with Jeff's bullshit sometimes in order not to feel invisible and alone."

"What's that mean?"

"When you have nothing and no one, there doesn't seem to be much of a point. No one would even miss me. I could disappear, and nothing would change for a single soul. The only people who cared died."

I'm speechless for maybe the first time in my life. I've never once had that thought. Never thought it wouldn't matter if I dropped off the face of the earth. My parents would be crippled with grief. My grandparents would be devastated. All the people in my life would feel some sort of emotion.

"I can't imagine," I whisper.

"So, sometimes it's better to be visible, even if you're not treated great all the time. At least you're seen. And I thought maybe he'd care if I died. But based on what happened last night and how quickly he filled my spot, I guess I was wrong." She turns her head, staring out the window that faces the backyard.

She looks so sad, and I want to do whatever I can to wipe away the feelings she's experiencing.

"I'm sure it would've been different if you'd died." I cringe immediately. The words were meant to be nice, but they came out sounding like the stupidest fucking shit in the entire world. "He's pissed right now, but who cares. He doesn't have any right to be mad when he's the one who treated you like shit."

She runs her index finger up and down the coffee mug,

her eyes fixed on the movement. "You know the worst part?"

"What's that?"

"I don't even care about the other girl—or him, for that matter. I'm not mad. I'm not even sad. I'm nothing."

"And that's bad, why?"

She tips her head back, staring me straight in the eyes. She doesn't look as frail as she did last night when we stood in the shop. "I should feel something, shouldn't I?"

"Nope. He isn't worthy of your sadness, but you should be pissed. Very pissed at the way he treated you."

Opal sighs and goes back to looking out the window. "I'm happy to be away from him. I lay in bed all night and thought about how peaceful I felt for the first time in as long as I could remember."

"Good. Everyone deserves some peace."

"I guess so," she whispers.

"I was serious earlier."

She turns her head toward me, giving me those beautiful blue eyes. "About what?"

"About staying here." My palms are sweaty because I've never lived with a woman, especially one I would sleep with in a heartbeat but haven't yet.

"You want to be roomies?" She has a small smile on her face.

"Yeah," I say, but my voice cracks a little when I answer. "For as long or as little as you like."

"As long as I like. You sure about that?"

I swallow, trying not to throw up. It's as if someone

else has possessed me because the man I was a few days ago would've never asked her to live with me.

"What if I'm a murderer?"

I laugh, shaking my head. "I'm still alive, and based on the look of you—" I let my eyes travel down her frame, "—I'm thinking I could take you."

"What if I'm a neat freak?"

I wave my hand around the kitchen, which is clean but not neat. "Clean your heart out."

"What if you want to bring a woman home?"

"I won't." I'm quick to answer.

"But what if you do? You're a handsome guy."

I smile at her words. "You think I'm handsome?"

Her cheeks turn a pretty shade of pink as she looks away from me. "You know you're handsome. Stop."

"Will you feel weird if you bring guys home?" I ask, hoping she'll say yes because the thought makes my blood boil.

Her eyes slice to mine. "I couldn't do that. That would be rude."

I tilt my head, studying her face. "Why?"

She shrugs and shifts her gaze away again. "It's a nice offer. A really great offer, actually, but I think it's best if I spend some time on my own again. I need to get my head right after what I've been through."

I nod. "Makes sense."

She lifts her coffee cup to her lips. "I'll look for places today," she says against the rim.

"If you need to stay another night, you're more than

welcome to use the guest room again. I'm not kicking you out."

Her eyes search my face as she places her coffee mug back on the table, but she keeps her hand wrapped around the base. "You're a good guy, Stone."

"Don't tell anyone."

"Why?"

"I have a reputation to uphold, and being good isn't something I'm known for."

"So, you're an asshole?"

"Sometimes."

"Is the asshole or this nice guy sitting next to me the act?"

"A little of both."

"Men are weird," she mutters, shaking her head.

"I'm not like most men." I lean back, stretching my legs out until they're straight. "I like to keep people guessing…curious, almost."

"I'll keep your secret."

I smile at her, wishing I could reach out and touch her cheek that looks as soft as silk. "Thank you."

She pushes her chair back and stands, taking her coffee mug with her. "I'm going to get dressed, and I'll be ready to go when you are."

"Give me ten."

She places her hand on my bare shoulder. "I'll pay you back for your kindness someday."

I peer up at her, soaking in her beauty. "There's no need, Opal. I'm happy I can help."

Her smile makes my heart stutter a little as she gives my shoulder a squeeze. I obviously need to get laid because even the lightest of touches shouldn't be affecting me the way it does.

I did my good deed for the year, and now I'm about to make every wrong decision to negate the shit out of it too.

6

OPAL

"Opal?" my boss calls from across the room.

I pop my head up over my cubicle divider, searching for her until my eyes land on her sour face. The woman never smiles and has perpetual resting bitch face. It wouldn't be an issue if her attitude didn't match her look so perfectly.

"Yeah?" I say softly, hating to be called out in front of other people.

The office has grown quiet, and while no one is looking at either of us, there's definitely a tense vibe. I haven't been here long enough to know what this means, but based on the reaction of the room, it's not good.

"Come into my office, please." She turns around, walking back inside her cramped and messy office, but leaves the door open.

"Sucks, man," the girl with bright-pink hair in the

cubicle in front of me mutters. "I'm sorry." Her smile is tight. "Keep your chin up."

I push away from my desk and stand. "What's it mean?" I ask her, my gaze moving from her pained face to the open door.

"You're getting canned."

"Canned, as in fired?"

The girl nods. "Every time."

Damn it. This is the last thing I need right now. I depleted much of my savings by staying in a hotel for a week while I found an apartment. Then there was the security deposit and first month's rent. Don't even get me started on all the little things and furniture.

I walk slowly, hoping if she has a few extra seconds to think that, somehow, it'll all end differently. My stomach gurgles, threatening to rid itself of all the things I ate for lunch. I place my hand on my belly and hope I can keep everything down while my boss fires me.

I step inside her office and wait near the door as she keeps her eyes trained on her screen and her fingers typing away at her keyboard.

"Sit," she commands.

My gaze moves away from her to the area across from her desk. There's no empty space. Papers are everywhere, including stacks of them on the two chairs opposite her desk.

"Or stand," she mutters when her eyes follow mine to the mess. "I hate to do this…"

I know what that means, and it's exactly as the pink-haired girl had predicted. Nothing good starts with "I hate to do this." Nothing.

"We're overstaffed, and since you're the last one hired, we're going to need to let you go. I'll make sure you're paid for the rest of the day, but your services are no longer needed."

"I don't even get to finish out the week?" I ask, twisting my fingers together in front of me as I start to think of new ways to make cash.

She shakes her head. "No, Opal. You'll get your eight hours today, and that's it. You were a good worker, and you could've become one of the best in the office."

I hold in my snort. This is a telemarketing company. It's the only place that would hire me immediately and require nothing from me besides a one-hour training course and a driver's license. They were the first to respond to my application online, and I took it because it was just something to earn cash while I found a real job.

"Well." I clear my throat, hating that I'm being fired but suddenly feeling a new sense of peace. "I appreciate you giving me a shot."

My now ex-boss gives me a little chin lift before moving papers around on her desk. "You can go now."

"Leave your office now, or leave *the* office now?"

"The office," she tells me. "Grab your stuff and go. My boss is coming in today, and he can't see you here."

"But won't he see my paycheck?"

She peers up at me, and her eyes move around like

she's thinking about something. "Good point. I can pay you for the rest of the hour but not the entire day."

Fuck. Way to go, Opal. I talked her out of paying me for the entire day in the blink of an eye. "Great," I mumble.

I stalk to my desk, grab my purse, and head for the door without a goodbye to anyone. In the short amount of time I'd worked at ABC Telemarketing, I hadn't bothered to make any friends. By the time our break rolled around, everyone was talked out and stayed glued to their own phone screens for downtime. Plus, I never thought I'd stay here long. Making calls to people who want nothing to do with whatever reason I'm calling isn't something I want to do as a long-term career.

As soon as I make it to my car, I pull out my phone and check my account balance. I take a deep breath, realizing I have a buffer that'll last me a few months at most.

I'm halfway to my apartment when steering my car becomes harder than normal. There's a bounce to the car, and I instantly break out in a cold sweat. I don't need this right now. Money's too tight to have my car take another shit on me after just getting it out of the shop a month ago.

I slow down so I don't do any more damage to whatever the hell is wrong with this worthless car and lean forward, searching all the street signs for the nearest mechanic.

My eyes land on *Nuts & Bolts*, and without hesitation, I pull into the parking lot. I place two hands on the steering wheel and sit inside my car, letting the air conditioning blast me in the face before I have to step out into the unforgiving Florida sun.

As soon as I'm outside my car, I see the issue. My front tire is flat. At least the problem isn't something more serious or expensive. My savings can't take a major hit right now.

The auto shop doesn't look like any of the other ones in the area. Its brightly painted exterior is eye-catching, which is necessary in an overcrowded market or on a busy street.

I grab the handle, flinging open the front door, and I am not prepared for what I find inside. The exterior is nothing compared to the glam waiting room, filled with oversize, comfortable chairs, bookshelves stocked with row upon row of books, and a radio playing soothing music. I'm frozen inside the doorway, taking in the awesomeness of the place.

A woman is sitting at the counter with a phone resting between her shoulder and ear as she types away on the computer. She makes eye contact with me and smiles, lifting a finger to tell me to hold on a second.

I take the time to walk by the bookshelves, scanning the titles in every genre imaginable. I could easily pull a half dozen books off the first shelf alone that I'd be able to escape into without a moment's hesitation.

"Hey," the woman says as soon as she hangs up the phone. "Sorry about that. It's been a busy day."

I move away from the mini library and head toward the desk. "No problem." I gaze toward my parked car, cursing it in my head. "I have a flat and was hoping to get it fixed."

"Sure. Sure. No problem." Her gaze moves back to the screen in front of her, and she punches away at a few buttons. "You got an hour or two? We're a little behind, but I think I can squeeze you in."

I don't have anywhere I have to be. I'd planned to work all day, but that went to shit in a heartbeat. "Sure. I'll wait." It's not like I have a choice. I can't drive around town to find someone who could fit me in this very second without risking doing more damage to my rim.

"You can make yourself comfortable while you wait. There's a coffeemaker around the corner and a mini fridge filled with drinks of all sorts."

"Wow. Okay," I say, wondering how I got so very lucky to land in a shop like this instead of the dirty places I've been to before.

"I need some information and your keys."

"How much will it be?" I ask her as I walk up to the counter with my car keys in my hand, praying it won't be more than a hundred dollars.

"It depends on if he can plug it or you need a new tire."

My shoulders sag forward, and like my tire, everything inside me deflates. "I can't afford a new tire right now," I say softly, hating to admit my inability to pay for something so basic.

The woman gives me a pained smile. "Let's wait until my husband takes a look. We'll figure it out from there, okay?"

INFERNO

"Yeah." I don't have a choice. I'm stuck here, and the ability to go anywhere else isn't an option. That would require a tow truck and even more money out of my pocket.

"Now, let me get you into the computer, and my husband will take a look."

The door to the garage area opens, and a man walks in, sucking all the air out of the room. His face is rugged and handsome at the same time, covered in streaks of grease. He has long hair that's tied back, and the parts of his body that are visible are covered in tattoos. His eyes meet mine for a moment, and I swear to God, my heart does a double beat.

"What do we got, princess?" he asks her, sliding an arm around her waist as she's propped up on a counter-height chair. He nuzzles her neck, burying his face in her hair.

She turns her head slightly to look at his face. "She has a flat. Repair would be optimal instead of replacement. Can you make that happen, baby?"

His lips touch her neck, and somehow, she doesn't melt into a puddle. When he turns his gaze my way, I have to tell myself to stay upright. "I'll do my best. Give me ten to take a look."

All I do is nod.

I don't know who's luckier—him or her. They're both stunning and madly in love with each other. Someday I'll find someone who looks at me the way he looks at her, but today isn't that day.

"Get to it, baby," she says to him, which is met with a low grunt before he peels away from her body. "I need to get your information."

The man walks up to me, and I tip my head back to get a better look at his face. Yep. Hotter up close, which I would've thought damn near impossible.

"Keys," he says, holding out his hand.

I swallow as I place my keys in his hand, still staring at his face. "Thanks."

"Welcome," he says before stalking away, twirling my key ring which holds exactly two keys—my apartment and my car.

As soon as the door to the garage closes and the man is gone, it's like the air inside the room changes.

"He's something else," she says to the computer screen, and I'm about to agree with her when her phone rings. She glances down, and her lips purse. "One sec." She taps the screen as she lifts the phone to her ear. "Hey, Ma. What's up?"

I move away from her desk, making myself appear to be busy studying the posters and artwork around the waiting room. I hate when people eavesdrop on my conversations, and I do my best not to do it to her.

"How bad is it?" she asks her ma and pauses. "Take off some of his layers and give him something cold to drink." Another pause and a sigh. "Yeah, Ma, a popsicle works too." Another pause.

I turn, seeing her listening intently, but also rolling her eyes.

"Yeah, you can take him in the pool. The water should cool him down. I'll leave the shop in a few minutes to get him." She raises a finger at me, and I feel bad about being caught watching her. "It's okay. I'll be there soon."

She hangs up her phone and lets out a loud sigh. "Sorry about that. Sick kid."

"Sucks," I mutter, but I really have no idea. I can't imagine having a kid and trying to work. Add in them being sick and it's a whole new complicated ball game.

"I only need your name and number for your file. Mammoth will finish up everything else when he's done checking your tire."

"Mammoth?"

She smiles at me as she types away on the keyboard. "My husband. The guy who was in here before."

The name is fitting, and I don't know who's luckier to be married to the other. "No problem. My name is—"

"Opal?" a woman calls out.

I spin around, finding the woman from the tattoo shop the night Jeff thankfully exited my life. "It's me," I say with a tight smile because, for the life of me, I can't remember her name.

She marches up to me, her arms wide. "Oh my God. It's so good to see you," she says, throwing those wide arms around my body to hug me. "I've thought about you more than a few times, and Stone and I talked about you."

Great. They've *talked* about me. What does that mean? No. Maybe I don't want to know.

"It's good to see you," I say, because what else does someone say at a time like this?

"You're Opal?" the woman asks from behind the desk. "*The* Opal?"

I don't know who *The* Opal is, but now, I'm guessing she's me. "I think so."

The tattoo-shop woman releases me from her tight embrace and turns her head toward the woman at the desk. "Tam, this is her. Stone's girl."

Stone's girl?

The woman behind the desk, who I now know as Tam, shoots straight up out of her seat. "No way. Un-fucking-believable. You're Stone's Opal?"

I shrug, confused.

"Gigi, this is crazy," Tam says to the woman who walked in.

"Totally bananas, Tam. What are the chances?"

The women stare at me, beaming with so much excitement and joy it almost vibrates off them.

"You need to tell him," Tam says.

Gigi shakes her head. "He'll lose his shit."

Stone called me a few times to check up on me, but nothing more has come from our talks. He helped me at a time when no one else would do the same. I liked Stone… liked him a little too much, but it was clear to me the feelings weren't mutual.

It has been weeks since the last time he called. I figured he moved on and forgot about me, but clearly, these two women think otherwise.

"He won't care," I tell them. "It's not a big deal."

Two wide-eyed women turn their heads in my direction.

"What are you talking about?" Gigi asks, her eyes back to normal but her eyebrows furrowed in confusion. "He won't care?"

I nod. "We're friends." I swallow, twisting my fingers together in front of me. "Or we were. He hasn't called in a while, so…"

"Girl," Gigi says, getting a little more animated. "That man is head-over-fucking-heels for you."

I blink. "He's head-over-fucking-heels for me?"

Tam laughs. "Never seen him so twisted over a chick." She tilts her head, studying me. "But now that I'm seeing her, I get it. She's got it."

"What's *it*?" I whisper, suddenly feeling like I'm under a microscope.

"The looks. The body. Everything is sheer perfection," Tam answers.

"I'm sure Stone doesn't have an issue with finding women who have good bodies and are pretty," I tell her.

Tam laughs. "You're not lying, but I never hear about them. You, though…" She shakes her head. "He hasn't stopped talking about you."

Weird.

He may be talking about me, but he isn't talking *to* me. "That's…" I don't know what to say. Is it nice? I guess it is.

"I have to text him and let him know you're here," Gigi says, pulling out her phone. "Is that okay?"

I shrug. It's not like he's going to drop everything and come running. What's the harm?

"Shit. I have to run. My mom called, and Riley's sick. She's in a panic like she's never dealt with a sick kid before."

Gigi snorts. "They've all lost their minds."

"Opal, Mammoth will be in shortly. Hang tight."

"Got it," I say to her as I move back toward a chair in the waiting area, keeping my eye on Gigi as she taps away at her phone screen.

"The alert has been sent," Gigi says before Tam's out the door.

"Damn. I miss all the good stuff. Text me what happens," she tells Gigi.

Gigi gives her a nod before sliding into a chair next to me. "You okay?"

"It's just been a shit day. I lost my job, and now—" I wave my hand toward the garage area "—I have a flat."

Gigi shakes her head and sighs. "I swear, sometimes it feels like life takes a giant shit on us all at once."

I lean back in my chair, trying not to think about Stone. "Yep. So, now I have to find a new job and hope I don't need a new tire to boot."

Gigi checks her phone as she taps her foot. "He must be busy. He hasn't replied."

"It's okay," I tell her, feeling all kinds of things. Relieved that he doesn't have to see me on another bad day, but also a little sad because he makes a dark day a little brighter. "He has a life."

"Want company?" she asks, checking her screen again. "I can stick around."

"No, babe. You go do your stuff. I'm going to enjoy a little solitude and try to figure out my next move."

"Stop by the shop sometime and say hi. Maybe you'd like a little ink. I'd be honored to be the one to do it for you."

"I may do that," I lie. I'm petrified of needles, and the thought of something permanent on my skin freaks me out.

She leans over and gives me a kiss on each cheek before heading toward the garage. "Don't be a stranger," she says with a smile and a wave.

I nod. "I won't." But I have no intention of going to the shop or trying to insert myself into their lives.

As soon as she's gone, I pick up my phone and search for my next job. It's time for me to make some solid plans for my future instead of just trying to survive.

7

STONE

My heart's pounding as I pull into Nuts & Bolts. I didn't even take the time to reply to Gigi's text before I hit the road, wanting to see Opal.

I've spent the last couple of weeks trying to play it cool, letting her be the one to initiate contact as much as possible.

But I know I want her, and she isn't moving as fast as I'd like.

The attraction is there.

The air sizzled around us, but at the time, she wasn't in the right headspace because of her douchebag ex-boyfriend.

I'm done waiting.

When I know what I want, I go after it.

And right now, it's Opal.

My truck isn't even fully parked when I spot her through the glass window in the waiting room. But she isn't alone. Her hands are moving around, and she's putting her entire body into the conversation.

I squint, trying to get a better look at who has her so animated.

When my eyes finally focus, fighting the sunshine and reflection, I lose my mind.

It's Jeff.

I'm out of my truck, hustling toward the door, ready to knock his ass out.

Has she been seeing him?

Did they get back together?

I stutter in my step for a moment, wondering if I should turn my ass around. Maybe I read our short time together completely wrong. Maybe after she found her own place, she decided to go back to him. Crazier shit has happened. Relationships are complicated and something I've avoided at all costs to avoid any type of bullshit.

"Fuck you!" Opal yells, her voice carrying through the glass of the customer area.

Jeff's eyes find me as I pull open the door, ready to take out the trash.

"How the hell did you even find me here?" Opal asks him, her hands balled up at her sides.

"Yeah. I'd like to know that too," I say, rushing into the waiting room to stand behind Opal.

She turns her head, and her eyes widen when they land on me. "Stone," she says in a quieter voice.

Mammoth stalks into the waiting room, wiping his hand with a red rag. "We've got a problem."

"Fuck," Opal barks. "Of course. What the hell else could go wrong today?"

She's spicy. I like this side of her. She doesn't seem like the meek and mild woman who was beaten down emotionally a few short weeks ago.

Mammoth looks at Opal, then to me, and lastly to Jeff. "What the..."

"Hey, man. What's the issue?" I ask my cousin.

He reaches into his pocket, pulling out what looks like a silver coin. "Found this on her car."

"Found what?" Opal and I ask in unison.

Mammoth holds the small thing in the air. "Looks like a tracking device."

Opal turns her full attention to Jeff, but before she can unleash on him, I step in front of her. "Lemme handle him, baby."

She reaches out, placing her hands on my arms, but doesn't do anything to stop me. "What a fucking asshole. You did this, didn't you?" she asks Jeff.

And since he is the only one who wasn't confused by what exactly was between Mammoth's fingers, I'd say it's pretty obvious he's the one who planted it.

"It wasn't me," Jeff replies, his lips pinched and arms crossed. "I didn't do shit."

I take a step forward, leaving only a few feet between him and myself. I'm not above knocking him out, even in my cousin's business. There is no better place for it to happen, actually. "How. The. Fuck. Did. You. Know. She. Was. Here?" My words are sharp and biting.

Jeff takes a step back, trying to avoid whatever I am about to fling his way. "I didn't put that there."

I move forward, leaving him nowhere to go except to plant his ass in the chair that's touching the backs of his knees. "You're not answering the question. I'll ask one more time, and then I'm busting your nose to start, until you confess."

Jeff leans back, bending in such an unnatural way, but definitely scared. Most men like him are. They can push a woman around and treat her like shit, but put even the smallest amount of pressure on them and they instantly turn into a pussy. "I was driving by and saw her in the window."

I raise an eyebrow and lean into his space, forcing him backward even farther.

"That's a crock of shit," Mammoth mutters from behind me. "Can't see shit going fifty down the road."

"Don't get arrested," Opal whispers behind me. "Please."

I growl, wanting nothing more than to punch his lights out. He deserves as much.

"It's a crime to plant a device like this."

"Call the cops," I bite out, hating that I'm not going to lay him out. "Let them deal with this trash."

Opal skates her fingertips across the bare skin on my upper arms. "Thank you," she says.

I bend my neck, so my nose is touching his. I stare into his beady dark eyes. "If I see you around her again, I'm breaking something on your body, and I don't give two shits if I end up in jail. Forget about Opal. You don't talk to Opal. You don't see Opal. She doesn't exist to you. You don't listen, you're going to feel more pain than you ever thought possible while staying conscious."

"You can't threaten me," he snaps.

I smile. "Did anyone hear me threaten him?"

"Nope," Opal says first, and I wish to fuck I could turn around. I'm pretty sure I would see a smile on her face.

"I didn't hear shit," Mammoth answers. "Hey, yeah. We have a situation at Nuts & Bolts over on Nineteen."

"Please," Jeff begs. "Hang up."

"If you could send a cruiser or five, that would be great," Mammoth says to the sheriff dispatch.

Jeff's almost shaking and falls backward into the chair, unable to keep himself balanced as I remain in his space. "I'll never call her again. I promise."

"This is some fucked-up shit, and I've seen a lot of fucked-up shit," Mammoth says. "If he doesn't keep you here, I sure as fuck am."

"Oh, I'm keeping him here."

Jeff's eyes dart toward the door.

"Nope," I snap, placing the entire pressure of my booted foot on top of his bare foot covered in a stupid sandal.

"Damn," Opal mumbles from behind me, but her soft hands never leave my skin.

Jeff cries out, lurching forward to reach for his foot, but I don't care. I think he's spent his life inflicting pain on other people, and for what may be the first time ever, he's about to experience a little payback.

I twist my boot, giving him a little something extra. "You're not running either."

"They'll be here in five," Mammoth tells us.

Jeff's red face immediately pales. "You don't know the whole story," he barely gets out as the pain from the weight of my entire six-foot-three body pushes down on the tiny bones of his foot.

"Why don't you enlighten me?"

"She's a lying whore, and she likes when I treat her like that."

With those words, I snap. I reach down and grab him by the neck, yanking him straight out of the chair and his sandal. "You've said too much, and now we're going to handle this portion of the day before the cops arrive."

He struggles against my hold, clawing at my wrist with his stubby fingers. "Opal, babe, where do you want me to hit him?" I ask her. "He's not getting away without at least one bruise." I study his face, watching his skin turn a bright shade of red. "Maybe two."

Opal's thumb caresses my triceps. "None, but if you have to do something…one."

"One it is," I reply to her before rearing back with my free hand, careful not to hurt her, and slam my fist right into his cheek.

The sound of his bones crunching against my knuckles will forever be burned into my memory. But I won't cringe when I remember the moment I sent Jeff to the floor, gasping for air and writhing in pain.

"You deserve worse," I tell him, nudging him with my boot as he rolls around on the floor like a fish out of water.

"The sheriff," Mammoth calls out in warning. "Three cars."

I turn around, instantly grabbing Opal around the waist and holding her tightly in my arms. "I'm sorry," I tell her as she tips her head back to stare up at me.

"Thank you," she breathes. "I don't know what I would've done if you hadn't shown up."

"Mammoth would've handled him. We got you, baby."

She melts into me, pressing her cheek against my chest. "I can't believe he showed up here and he's been tracking me. It's just so…so… Gah. I don't even know what it is."

"It's scary as fuck," I mutter into her hair. "But it won't happen again. He's behind you and will never bother you again. I'll make sure of that, Opal."

"What's going on?" the first officer asks as he walks through the door, hand on his holstered gun.

Mammoth makes his way across the waiting room, holding the tracker in his hand. Opal and i stay glued together as Mammoth goes over what he found on Opal's car and where exactly he found it.

"Ma'am, do you have any idea who would've planted that on your car?"

Opal barely peels her body away from mine to give her

attention to the law enforcement officer. "Him," she says, jutting her chin out toward Jeff. "He's my ex-boyfriend. He showed up here today out of the blue, and I couldn't figure out how he found me until the mechanic showed us the device."

"He didn't have consent to place the device on your vehicle?" the officer asks her, ignoring Jeff as he lies on the floor, moaning in pain.

Fucking baby.

"No. I didn't give him consent, and I didn't know it was on there."

"He's been verbally abusive to her." I add to the conversation because I want them to understand exactly what kind of garbage they're dealing with.

"We see this more and more," the guy tells us as his backup bends over, lifting Jeff off the floor. "We'll need to take the device into evidence and have you come down to the station to file a complaint. Are you feeling up to it?"

"He hit me," Jeff says, one side of his face already turning a beautiful shade of purple. "Arrest him."

"Zip it," the officer tells Jeff. "You're the only one going to jail today, buddy. Save your breath."

"This is bullshit," Jeff seethes, struggling with the guys as they place him in handcuffs.

"We can either do this the easy way or the hard way."

Jeff grunts his displeasure at the entire situation, but no one pays him any attention or gives two shits which way they put him in handcuffs.

"Does she need to go to the station immediately?" I ask the officer.

"Take your time. He's not going anywhere anytime soon. Processing and such will take a few hours."

I give the guy a chin lift.

"I'll need to take that," one of the guys says to Mammoth, holding out a tiny plastic bag for the tracking device.

"Figured as much."

"We'll need a statement from you too."

"You got it."

"Out you go," the officer says, hauling Jeff out the door as he yells at the top of his lungs about what a crock of shit the entire thing is.

I slide my hands up to Opal's arms. "You okay?"

She peers up at me and lets her body lean into mine. "I am now," she breathes against my shirt. "I am now."

8

OPAL

"Babe, feet," Stone says as soon as we sit down on my couch. He pats his lap with both hands and stares at me. "You've had a long day."

I blink and take a moment to let his words and actions wash over me. "What?" I ask, because no matter how many seconds I take to process what's happening, I can't quite believe the reality.

"You deserve a little relaxation. Give me your feet. I'll rub the tension out of you."

I want to tell him that something else could be rubbed that's an even better stress-reliever, but I keep that thought to myself.

I raise my eyebrows, genuinely surprised by the kindness he's shown me over and over again. "Are you messing with me?"

"No." He pats his thighs again, drawing my gaze to his crotch.

I do my best to look away before he notices, but damn if I didn't get a good look at the outline of his dick. And as far as I can tell, the man is big everywhere. I lean back slowly, sliding across the couch until my feet are near him. He does the rest, closing his thick fingers around my foot, pulling me toward him.

"Close your eyes."

He's bossy, but honestly, I don't even mind. I'm used to bossy people in my life, but usually it's not to my benefit.

I press the back of my head into the pillow, willing my eyes to stay open. I stare down the length of my body, soaking in his appearance from the side.

His features are sharp and unique. Dark brown hair with a slight curl to the longer pieces. Clearly, he needs a haircut, but he's still handsome with the messy strands. His dark-green eyes remind me of the Pacific Northwest with its tall pine trees and moody rain. His lips are full, totally made for kissing as far as I can tell without testing my theory personally.

When his thumb presses into the bottom of my foot and he starts to knead my sore muscles, I moan softly and let my eyes flutter closed completely.

Fuck. This is so damn good. I don't remember if anyone's rubbed my feet unless I paid them to do it. No one's ever offered to do it for me to relieve my stress, but it's definitely something I could get used to having more often.

"Thanks for today," I whisper, trying to hide the pleasure in my voice. "I don't know what I would've done without you."

"It's a messed-up situation."

"Yeah," I breathe.

His upper arms are almost the size of my thighs, and I feel every ounce of their power as he rubs my feet.

"I'm going to stay here for a few days."

My eyes snap open and land on him. "What?"

He nods slowly but keeps his gaze on what he's doing. "Jeff's going to get released and be more pissed off. I think it's best if I camp out on your couch until we see if he's going to try to make contact."

"But the restraining order."

He moves his fingers to my heels, and my eyes roll back in my head. He's playing dirty. "I have a feeling a guy like Jeff doesn't give two shits about a piece of paper."

"I have a bat if he tries anything."

Stone's body tightens underneath my legs, which are resting on his massive thighs. "Opal, what the hell are you going to do with a bat?"

"Hit him," I state plainly because, duh, what else would I do with a bat?

Stone turns the weight of his gaze toward me without a hint of a smile. "And when he takes it from you?"

I shrug a shoulder, not having the energy for much else. "He won't."

"You want to test this theory of yours?"

"No."

"You're better off with pepper gel than a bat."

I wrinkle my nose. "I don't think so."

Stone's eyes roll back ever so slightly. "Women," he sighs. "You're very hardheaded."

"I'm not, but maybe your other women are." Internally, I cringe immediately after saying those words. His *other* women. Does that infer that I'm one of his women?

"I don't have other women, just you. And there isn't a woman in my life who isn't hardheaded, and I'm surrounded by them."

"The bat will work," I say, not wanting to talk about the women in his life. I know he's not being truthful. A man doesn't look like Stone and not have a group lusting after him at every turn.

He stops rubbing my feet. "Do you have a bat?"

I tick my chin toward my front door, where one is resting in the corner.

"It's wood."

"Well, yeah." I push myself up and pull my feet back, turning my body into a seated position. "Of course. Only the best."

Stone grunts. "The worst type for what you're trying to do."

"You ever been hit by one?"

He shakes his head. "You ever swung one?"

I nod. "When I was younger, I played softball."

"You think you can swing that fast enough to inflict pain on someone before they can stop you?"

I glance at the bat and then back at him, confident in my ability. "Yep."

He's instantly on his feet, moving toward my front door. "Let's test it, then." He reaches down and grabs the bat, making the handle look minuscule in his big hand. "Come on."

Shit. This is the last thing I wanted to do tonight. I was really enjoying the foot rub, but I had to open my big mouth. And Stone, being the man he is, has to prove a point. One which he'll ultimately lose. "Fine," I say, propelling myself off the couch and toward the door. "I have no problem making you eat your words, big man."

He smirks. "Want to make it interesting?"

I stalk up to him, hands on my hips, ready to show him how right I am. "What do you have in mind?"

He rubs his chin with his fingers, taking a few seconds to think of all the options. "If I'm right and you can't hit me, I get to kiss you."

My eyes flash, not because I don't want to kiss him, but because I'm surprised he wants to kiss me. "Lame," I mutter. "You could've asked for something bigger."

Stone steps into my space, filling the air with his scent and the heat from his body.

It takes everything in me not to reach out, grab his big, bulky arms, and plant my lips on his mouth. I wanted to throw myself around him after what happened with Jeff. I'd never felt more protected in my entire life than in that moment.

Stone raises an eyebrow. "You want to go bigger?"

My knees weaken, but I somehow remain standing. I want to scream yes because I've had a dry spell bigger than the Sahara. "A kiss works."

Stone's lips turn up. "You're a big talker, little girl."

"And what do I get if I'm right?"

He leans his head down closer until I can feel the warmth from his breath. "What do you want?" he asks, pinning me with his green eyes and making me go stupid for a second.

I want everything.

I want skin on skin. I want lips on lips. I want him…all of him. I want to know what it's like to be loved by a man like Stone. I want to know what he sounds like when he has an orgasm. Is he a moaner or is he silent?

I have so many questions and things I want to know about him, but damn, he's putting me on the spot.

I stare straight into his green eyes, showing no fear. Just say it, Opal. "An orgasm."

He jerks his head back slightly, and his eyebrows rise. "Yeah?"

"Yep," I clip out. "A big one."

"I didn't expect you to say that. Damn, Opal."

I keep my gaze on him, not wavering in the slightest on the outside, but inside, I'm a freaking mess. What in the hell got into me? I've never been this woman until now. "Worried you can't make it happen?" I challenge him. "Most men can't find the…"

His eyes darken as he brings his face close to mine. "I know how to make you come, Opal," he whispers, making the hair on my arms stand on end. "I'm debating whether I should let you hit me because I want to taste you more than I want to breathe. But that would require me not proving my point and you having a false sense of security."

"It sounds like you have a conundrum there, big man. Decisions, decisions," I tease.

"Either way, I win," he assures me with a salacious smile.

"I don't see how I'm losing either," I tell him.

He brings his face closer, our lips almost touching. I can't stop staring into his green eyes, captivated by the deep green color. "I'd rather lick your pussy than kiss your lips, but you're right, they're both a win-win. Though, now I'm thinking I've should've gone bigger with my prize."

My already-weak knees start to buckle, and it takes everything in me to stay standing. I'd rather him lick my pussy too, but I'm not getting into it now. "Enough talking. Are we doing this or what?" I ask, taking the bat from his hand and trying to ignore the sudden fire in my body.

It's not just a small fire; it's a full-fledged inferno.

Stone sucks in a deep breath before he pulls his upper body back and steps away. "I'm going to come through the door, and you try to knock my ass out."

"You sure you want me to give it my all?"

He laughs. "Babe, you can't hurt me. Give me everything you got."

"You're going to let me hit you?"

He shakes his head. "I have no doubt that orgasm you

crave isn't too far away, whether I win the bet or you do," he says, then turns around and walks out the front door.

"Fuck," I hiss into the air, staring at the closed door.

He's right, though. I'm damn sure the orgasm isn't too far away either, based on the way we've been staring at each other.

I take a deep breath, backing up a few steps before hauling the bat over my shoulder. Bending at my knees, I ready myself for the swing of a lifetime. My body's shaking, scared as hell that I'm going to hurt him and anything that's between us will evaporate in a split second.

"Don't be a pussy," he says through the door. "I want you to pretend it's Jeff walking through this door and not me."

My blood turns cold at the mere mention of that asshole. "Got it," I call back, tightening my grip on the tape-wrapped handle. "Bring it, big man."

The door starts to open, and I rear back on one foot, ready to swing, hoping I don't kill the guy. He's so nice, and it would be impossible to explain to the cops exactly what transpired here and how stupid we were.

Stone moves quicker than I expect, and I swing, barely making it halfway before his hand closes around the end of the bat, pulling it from my grip.

"See?" he says, sounding all smug.

I'm instantly deflated. One, I'm going to miss out on an orgasm, and two, my plan didn't work. Imagine if Jeff had tried to break in to my place? What a freaking mess.

"Yeah. You were right," I say flatly, dropping my hands to my sides, ready to plop my ass back on the couch.

I don't make it two steps away before the bat falls to the floor and Stone wraps his hand around my wrist. He hauls me backward like I weigh nothing at all.

"Not so fast," he says, pulling me to his chest with very little difficulty. "You have a debt to pay."

I tip my head up, closing my eyes and puckering my lips. I wait and wait, but nothing happens. I open my eyes, looking at his face. "What are you doing? Kiss me."

Stone's full lips turn up at one side as he slides his arms around my waist, sliding a hand up my spine to my hair. "I want to do it right," he tells me, his voice husky and deep.

I melt into his touch, the warmth and hardness of his body. He bends his neck, bringing his face closer, and I close my eyes right before his lips touch mine.

A sizzle of electricity shoots from my lips, down my body, and my knees wobble again. Stone's strong arms and frame support me, holding me upright, keeping me tight against him.

I feel him everywhere on my body as his lips move with mine. They're softer than I imagined, but somehow hard and demanding as he kisses me. I move my hands to his arms, sliding them up the muscular path to his shoulders. I press my breasts against his chest until there's no space between us.

He kisses me like I've never been kissed before. His teeth pull at my lower lip, nipping at the delicate flesh, sending a jolt of pleasure and pain through my entire system.

I don't know how long this goes on, but when his hand, that had been on my lower back, moves down to my ass, I can't stop myself from lifting my leg and snagging him around the waist.

"I want you," he murmurs against my lips, kneading my ass with one hand and grinding that big, thick cock into my middle.

"I want you too," I whisper into his mouth, my body answering instead of my brain.

We're doing this.

I'm doing this.

A million things run through my mind in a split second, but not a single one of them matters when he tangles his hand in my hair, pulling my head back to expose my neck.

As soon as his lips touch my throat, I get lost in the moment, forgetting every worry.

Everything around us disappears, and I let go, giving in to whatever is about to happen. I've spent too much time lately overthinking everything, including the attraction I've felt for Stone since the first night I spent at his house.

The need we feel for each other turns into a frenzy of kisses and hands pulling at clothes, leaving a trail of our shirts, pants, and anything else from the front door through the living room.

Stone guides me through the room, his mouth attached to mine and our limbs tangled around each other. When the backs of my knees touch the couch, I fall backward, bringing him with me.

I trail my fingertips over the muscles of his back, exploring all the hard ridges underneath his smooth skin. Stone's body is a work of art. I could spend a lifetime touching every square inch and never get bored.

"Wait," I say, my words coming out in a rush.

Stone lifts his head, staring down at me with punch-drunk eyes. "What's wrong?"

I press my palms against his pecs, loving the hardness in my hands. "Condoms. We need condoms."

"Plural?" A lazy smile spreads across his face. "I like your style, Opal."

I laugh. The man is truly impossible. "At least one."

He shakes his head. "Baby, once isn't going to be nearly enough."

My entire body is vibrating with anticipation of having sex with Stone at least once. I don't want to lie here, underneath him, planning out the rest of the evening. "Do you have them or not?"

He pushes himself up, and I watch in sheer wonder at the beauty of his body.

Holy hell.

The man is absolute perfection.

The ink is an added bonus. I didn't think I was much into tattoos, but seeing how they're placed on Stone's body has my mouth watering to trace every outline with my tongue.

"Don't move," he says to me, pointing down at the

couch like I'm about to trot off somewhere in my completely naked state.

"I'm not going anywhere, but if you don't get your ass in gear, I'm going to come without you." I move my hand between my legs and start to touch myself.

Stone's eyes widen, and his lips part. "Fuck me," he whispers, his cock bobbing in appreciation of the show I'm putting on in front of him. "You wouldn't dare."

I smirk and work my fingers more skillfully over my clit, touching myself the way I often do when I masturbate.

Stone's tongue darts out and sweeps across his lips as he stands as still as a statue. "This is…is…" He swallows as he gazes down at me.

I open my legs a little farther, giving him a better view, hoping he'll move faster. "This is hot, but your mouth would be hotter."

As soon as those words are out of my mouth, Stone drops to his knees and pushes my legs even farther apart. His mouth is on me a moment later, devouring the sensitive skin I've been touching.

"This is mine," he murmurs against my body, licking and sucking like he's been starving to get a taste of me.

I stare down my body as I tangle my fingers in his brown hair, finding his gaze on me.

I tear my eyes away from his, the intensity of his stare too much for me. Everything is heightened. The heat of his hand on my inner thigh, the warmth of his tongue against my skin, the low hum of excitement emanating from his lips as they're pressed against me.

He works my body like he's known it his entire life. Sucking, licking, and touching just the right spots to drive me so close to the edge, every toe on my foot starts to curl against the hardwood floor, and the familiar surge of pleasure crawls up my spine.

"Stone," I gasp, barely able to form words and catch my breath.

"Let go, Opal," he says, sending vibrations from his voice across my clit. "Come for me."

I didn't need the permission or his words to send me over the edge. The work of his fingers against my flesh and his tongue against my core has me panting through one of the most intense orgasms I've ever felt in my entire life.

My body seizes along with my breath. I can't think about anything other than the warm tingling that's coursing through every fiber of my being, sucking away my soul.

Stone doesn't let up or pull away; he doubles down by licking faster, sucking harder than he was before. I moan through the pleasure, expelling the air I've been holding in my lungs. I clamp my thighs together, trapping his head against me as I rock through the final pulses of ecstasy.

My body goes limp, every muscle spent and satisfied as I try to catch my breath. "Fuck," I breathe out with my eyes closed.

"That was hot as fuck," he says with his face still so close that I can feel the heat of his breath against my skin. "I want another."

I snap my eyes open. "I need time," I tell him, trying to

sit up, but my arms are still like jelly.

"Time?" He raises an eyebrow, looking so damn proud of himself. And he should be proud. That orgasm deserves a standing ovation, and I'd give him one if I had the ability to use my legs, which I don't. "Did I suck the life out of you?"

I smile down at him, the remnants of my pleasure glistening on his beautiful lips. "You did."

In my other life, before I met him, I wouldn't have been so forward. But there's something about Stone that makes me feel confident and not the least bit ashamed of being honest about everything, including sex.

He stands up, his cock harder and somehow looking larger than it did before. "I'll give you five minutes, and then I'm going back for seconds."

I can't take my eyes off his dick. It's a spectacular specimen. Straight, long, and thick. The most perfect combination and possibly the most beautiful one I've ever seen. My feelings for him are probably clouding my judgment of his member, but it doesn't matter... I want him in me.

"Fuck me," I tell him, my voice sounding needy and wanton. "I want to feel you inside me."

He tilts his head, looking impressed with me and himself. "My girl isn't satisfied. Insatiable," he whispers.

I don't argue. Although I'm more than satisfied, my body aches to be filled by him. "Only for you."

He turns on his heel, stalking toward his discarded pants in the entryway. I watch in a trance as his perfect ass gets smaller the farther away he goes. It's pure muscle, flexing with every step.

"Fuck," I whisper to myself, wondering how I got so damn lucky to end up with a guy like Stone. "He's hot as fuck."

"I heard you!" he yells from the front door.

I laugh softly, covering my mouth with my hand. Of course he heard me. He seems to hear and know everything, especially if it's a compliment.

When he marches back to me, he's rolling a condom over his hard length. "You sure you want this?" By this, I know he's not only talking about his cock, but himself too.

"I want all of it. All of you."

Something crosses his face, a look I can't quite place and haven't seen before. But a moment later, he's between my legs again.

"There's no coming back from this," he says to me as he lines up his cock at my entrance.

I reach up, placing my hands on his shoulders. "Take me, Stone. Do it. Do me. I want to feel you inside me."

The corners of his lips turn up before they cover mine, kissing me deeply as he pushes inside me at such a slow pace, I find it impossible to breathe. I brace myself for the quick, exquisite tinge of pain as my body gets used to his size.

He moans as he fully seats himself, plunging his tongue into my mouth. In that instant, I am totally consumed and owned by Stone Gallo, and I know I will never be the same.

9

STONE

"Looking kind of rough there, buddy." Pike smashes his shoulder into mine as he gives me a shit-eating grin. "Been a while since I've seen you so beat-up."

"Shut up," I grumble as I disinfect my station.

"Baby bro, what's wrong?" Lily asks as she plops down onto a stool next to mine. "Pike isn't lying. You look…"

I don't even look at my sister. I'm not giving her any ammunition to pry into my life. She's done that enough over the last twenty-odd years. "Don't you start."

"What? I didn't do anything. I'm just worried about you," she says.

Lily is always kind. The woman doesn't have a mean bone in her body. Even when we were growing up, she was nice. She never teased me or laid a hand on me, but if she had, I would've deserved it. I was a little shit compared to my angelic sister.

Lily rolls her stool closer to me. "I heard about what happened yesterday at Nuts & Bolts."

Of course she did. There are no secrets in this family, especially between my cousins. Word spreads faster than a wildfire when the brush is dry.

"Is Opal okay?" Lily touches my arm, trying to get my attention, although she already has it.

"Yep," I snap. "She's great."

And she is, but I'm not sure I am. Not because I don't like Opal, but because I like her *too* much. I've never been so interested in someone, and that scares the ever-living shit out of me. I'm drawn to her at the same time as I want to run away and bury my head in the sand in order to ignore my feelings that I know are coming hard and fast.

"And?" Lily pushes.

"And what?" I'm grumpy. Something I rarely am, and if I wasn't throwing off vibes before, I sure as fuck am now.

"Are you worried?"

Worried about my feelings. "Nope. He's behind bars."

"He may get out," Lily adds.

I turn to face my sister, who immediately smiles. "He didn't get bail. He's behind bars until his court date."

"Phew," she blows out, relaxing her shoulders. "That's good."

"Yeah."

"She has to be freaked out, though."

"She's okay," I reiterate. "At least Mammoth found the

device before Jeff had a chance to do something bad. She's relieved."

"That punk needs a taste of his own medicine," Gigi says as she walks by my station. "He needs more than that, but a little beating is good in my book."

Pike leans back in his chair, staring at his wife. "You going to do it, Rocky?"

Gigi laughs, pushing her hair behind one shoulder. "I could."

Pike bursts into laughter. "Darlin', you punch like a—"

"Say it," Gigi says, lifting her chin like she's about to throw down with him. "Go ahead. Light that firecracker." Her face is so serious, but just like Pike, I can't hold in my amusement.

She spins on her heel to face me, and I immediately sober, trying to force my face to stay emotionless. "You got something to say?"

I lift my hands, not trusting myself enough to speak. The last thing I want is my cousin pissed at me, and if I say anything about women being the weaker sex, she isn't the only one in the shop who will form a line to beat my ass.

"You better walk that back, big guy," Rebel tells Pike with her hands on her hips, looking no happier than Gigi.

"Baby," Pike says in a loving tone, trying to defuse the situation. "I know you can kick some major ass."

Gigi's tapping her high black boots, glaring at her husband. "But…"

"No buts," Pike tells her, shaking his head. "Weren't we talking about Stone and Opal?"

I narrow my eyes at the sellout. "Asshole," I mumble.

"Did you stay with her at the police station?" Lily asks, falling for Pike's redirection.

"Yeah."

"Longer?"

"Maybe."

Lily gasps. "You slept with her, didn't you?"

I don't answer right away, which is as telling as coming right out and saying yes.

"He's shot," Pike says from the other side of the room. "Dude's a goner. Look at him."

Gigi, Lily, and Rebel stop moving and stare at me. I can feel the weight of their gazes as they study my face for any sign of what I feel inside.

"I slept with her. Happy?" I turn my stool around to hide my face, hating the way they're looking at me like I'm an exhibit at a sideshow. "I've slept with plenty of women."

"You think he's a goner?" Gigi asks to the room.

"You ever see him this way?" Rebel adds.

"No," Lily answers. "Typically, he's high-fiving himself over his performance."

"That's not true," I grumble, but it's not a lie either. My skills even impress me sometimes. Even on my worst day, I'm better than most men with their mediocre ability to make a woman orgasm.

Lily slides her stool to the other side of my station,

leaning over so she can see my face. "Stone, it's okay if you like her. It's nothing to be ashamed of."

That's what she doesn't get.

I'm not ashamed. I'm fucking petrified.

This is uncharted territory for me. I've already spent more time with Opal than I have with anyone else who isn't related to me and has a pair of breasts.

And the really fucked-up thing is, I'm sitting at work, thinking only about her and wanting to be with her. I want to protect her and make sure she's okay. Who does that? A man who's so damn pussy-whipped he can't focus on anything else. And right now, that man is me.

I stop moving, dropping the cleaning rag on top of the table. "Why would I be ashamed, Lily?"

Lily shrugs with a crooked smile. "I'm just saying, it's okay."

I lean back, stretching my arms wide, trying to work out whatever stress is in my body. "Is it, though?"

Lily's nod is quick. "Yeah. Of course."

"I'm not ashamed," I repeat.

Lily scoots closer to my table, leaning her upper body over the top. "No, baby brother. You're not. You're falling in love."

"Am not," I bark, snapping forward until my forearms are on my knees. "I don't even know what love feels like."

Jett walks up next to my sister, placing his hand on her shoulder. "Baby, maybe he needs some time to process everything."

"There's nothing to process."

"Man, you got a lot to process," Jett tells me. "And when you come to whatever realization you're working through, you're going to be a bigger fucking mess."

"Don't you people have somewhere to be?" I ask all of them. "The shop closed a half hour ago."

My last appointment went longer than I scheduled. My family should've been long gone, but nope, they had to stay to ask me a bunch of questions and be nosy as hell.

"We wanted to stay to talk to you," Lily tells me.

"Lucky me," I mumble.

"Who wants to stop for a bite to eat?" Gigi asks. "I'm starving."

"Count me out," I say, wanting some time alone and not to continue the line of questioning about my feelings and personal life.

"You're such a baby," Rebel teases me.

"I'm meeting Asher for a drink."

"Where?" Lily asks. "We'll go there."

"They don't serve food."

Gigi narrows her eyes at me. "Why do you have to lie?"

I shrug. "I need some time to process shit without you all chirping in my ear."

"Yep. He's a goner," Pike states. "Ride that wave, brother. It's a great feeling."

"I feel like shit."

"Your body is in shock. It'll change. You'll be riding the wave of good feelings soon enough."

I pin my cousin with my gaze, hating his smug face sometimes. "You're full of shit."

Pike wraps his arm around Gigi's waist, pulling her closer until she's flush against his side. "I've never been happier. I never thought I'd get married, but boom, best thing to ever happen to me."

I hold back the vomit that's crawling up my throat at the thought of little ones running around my house. "You're living the dream...just not my dream."

"You'll see," Rebel says, rubbing her fingers in my hair to drive me crazy. "You'll get the kid bug and be the best dad."

"I'll be a kick-ass dad, but I'm not ready for all that picket-fence shit."

"No one is," Pike says, but I ignore him and his cheery outlook on relationships and love. "But you figure it out."

"I'm too young."

Everyone in the room laughs at my statement. I know it's stupid, but it's how I feel. I'm not old and not old enough to settle down.

"Time's ticking," Lily adds with a smile. "You're not getting any younger."

"Man, you people are rough today." I go back to cleaning my table, already having finished the rest of my workstation. "I'll let you know when I need you to know anything."

"Which is never," Rebel says. "You're like the Fort Knox of emotions."

"He doesn't have any, or at least he didn't until now,"

Gigi teases as she steps away. "The boy is in for a world of hurt."

"I hate you all," I call out as my cousins sit around laughing at my absurdity.

Pike stands and stretches. "I'm telling you now, brother, if you like her—like really, really like her—you lock that shit down and lock it down quick."

"Lock it down?" I ask, confused by his statement.

"Yep. Make sure she knows she's yours, or else someone else will snatch her away and you'll be there holding your dick and all alone."

"Ridiculous," I mumble.

"Women aren't going to wait around forever for you to come to your senses. If you don't snatch her up, someone else will."

"Noted," I tell him, giving him a salute because I'm a complete shithead and I don't want advice from anyone.

"He'll fuck it up," Lily says, pushing herself up from the stool before grabbing her purse. "He always does when it comes to feelings. He's allergic."

"Deathly," Gigi adds. "But what guy isn't at his age?"

I throw my rag in the dirty basket, ready to get the hell out of here and away from the conversation. "I'm out."

Lily pops up on her toes, giving me a kiss on my cheek. "Go get her," she whispers in my ear.

"Lily," I warn.

She pulls back and smiles at me. "Just let go, little brother. You won't be sorry."

"I already am," I whisper back.

"Where are we going?" Lily asks the rest of the group as I stalk toward the back, snapping off my latex gloves before tossing them in the trash can. I don't care where they go as long as it's not the Neon Cowboy.

"Where's Olive?" I ask Asher. His girl is never far behind him.

He exhales, leaning back in his chair with an exasperated look on his face. "She packed her shit and left."

My eyebrows rise. "What the hell did you do?"

"It's what I didn't do." He shakes his head and mumbles under his breath. "I fucked up."

"Shocker." I laugh. My cousin and I are the biggest fuckups of the family when it comes to women. "Now what? You going to let her go?"

He shrugs before taking a pull from his beer bottle. "I don't know what to do, man. Maybe we need space."

I pick at the cold fries in the middle of the table we'd decided to share to help wash down the lukewarm beer. "You trying to convince yourself of that? You don't sound sold on that bullshit."

"Don't you think we're too young for relationships?"

"Ash, you're asking the wrong man. You know my answer."

"I heard about Opal."

"I'm not even a little surprised." I lean forward,

turning the beer bottle in my hand. "Everyone's so damn nosy."

Asher laughs as he runs his fingers through his dark hair. "It's a pain in the ass, but they mean well."

I stare at him. "You're lying a lot tonight, asshole. You hate their gossip as much as I do."

"Only when it hits a little too close to home. Now, tell me what's happening with the chick."

I sigh and start to pick at the torn label on the brown bottle. "I don't know. I like her. I more than like her, but I don't know if I'm ready for more."

"Is she ready for more?"

I blink, staring at him. "Fuck. I didn't even ask."

"Dummy." He laughs as he reaches for a fry, giving one a squeeze. "Is it too much to ask for warm fries with a little crispiness to them?"

"It's the Neon Cowboy. We're lucky it's even edible."

"You really like this chick," he says, watching my face as closely as our family at the shop earlier.

I shrug again. "I do. More than I really want to."

He smiles at me, nodding. "Been there. It's scary as fuck."

"Terrifying. I mean, look at you. You're a mess. That's what relationships do, and I don't know if I'm ready to fuck up my life like that just yet."

Asher laughs again. "Stone, man, by the way you're talking, I'd say it's already too late."

"Fuck me," I groan.

"Is she that mint?"

"Yeah, man. Primo."

"Maybe you like being the hero."

I growl. "I'm not a hero."

"You saved her."

"She would've come to her senses eventually."

"Maybe or maybe not." He lifts his hand, holding up two fingers to the waitress when she looks our way. "Doesn't matter now. You changed her life."

"Have you ever known me to be a hero?"

He laughs. "Not unless there's something you want in the end. Maybe you already knew you wanted Opal and put things into motion to make it happen."

I look at him like he has three heads. "I barely got a look at her when it happened."

"And the second time?" He tilts his head, gazing at me intently with one raised eyebrow. "Yesterday."

"Fuck," I grumble, wiping my hand across my chin. "This is messed up."

"What's the problem? I heard she's beautiful."

"She is," I tell him, scratching at my overgrown facial hair. "I don't bang ugly chicks."

He shakes his head, but he talks the same way I do. "So, you slept with her. Now what? You going to cut her loose or lock her down?"

I roll my eyes. "You need to stop talking to Jett and Pike."

"I think it was Mammoth who said those words to me."

"Whatever."

He leans forward, pushing the shitty fries to the side. "Well…"

I shrug both shoulders, feeling more confused than I've ever been in my life. "I don't know."

"How will you feel if she walks out of your life and you never see her again."

My stomach twists into a tight knot at the very thought of her disappearing into nothingness. "That would suck."

"And if she sticks around, you guys date, and maybe eventually get married?"

My upper lip curls as I growl under my breath. "Shut up."

"Pussy," he teases. "How would you feel?"

"Asher, I'm scared shitless."

"Of what?"

"What if she's the one and the life I've always known is over?"

He nods because if anyone understands me, it's my cousin Asher. We've been thick as thieves forever. We were a terrible threesome until Trace got his balls all twisted and ended up with his ass married. "I got you. We can't stay shitheads forever, though. We need to grow up eventually."

"We do?"

He waves his hand across the table, pretending to smack me. "You're a jackass."

"You're the one taking a break from a kick-ass chick."

"I'm going to give her twenty-four hours before I

chase after her and beg for forgiveness. You haven't lived until you'd have makeup sex."

"Don't try to sell me on relationships. I can't trust you either. You're just like the rest of them."

He rolls his eyes. "I would never lie to you. If you have even a sliver of feelings for her, don't sell yourself short. Chase after her. Make her yours."

"I've never chased anyone before."

"Maybe that's why you like her so much."

"It's fucked up."

"You keep saying that, but you're the one making it more complicated than it is. You're not asking her to marry you right now, jagoff. Date the chick for a little while and then figure your shit out."

"Date only her?"

He sighs. "God, you are an idiot."

I give him my middle finger.

The waitress sets two beers on the table and wanders off before we can even say thank you.

Asher grabs his bottle, tilting it toward me. "A toast," he says, waiting for me to grab mine. When I do, he continues, "To growing up and falling in love."

I glare at him, not bothering to tap my bottle to his. "You're still an asshole."

"You're salty when you're in love."

"I'm not in love."

"Uh-huh," he mutters, smirking behind the lip of his bottle.

I can't be in love. I barely know her.

I'm in lust.

That's all it is, and it'll wear off quickly.

Maybe I need a few more tastes before she works her way out of my system and I can continue with my carefree and uncomplicated life.

10

OPAL

"Hello," I say cautiously into the phone after picking up a number I don't recognize.

"Opal?" the woman replies. The voice is familiar yet not.

"Yeah," I whisper and hold my breath.

"It's Fran. Stone's great-aunt. We met at the Neon Cowboy."

I exhale, feeling a sense of relief and joy at the sound of her cheery voice. I loved her from the moment I met her. She was like a breath of fresh air.

"Fran. Oh my God. Yes. How are you?"

"I'm as good as I can be at my age. I'm vertical, as they say. How are you, dear? How's Stone?"

I collapse back onto my couch. "I'm doing okay. Looking for work, and I have my own place now."

"And Stone?" she asks when I leave out a response about him on purpose.

"He's well, but I'm sure you know that."

"You two a thing yet?"

"I don't think so." I stare up at my ceiling, remembering all the things we did a few nights ago.

It was wonderful. The best I've ever had, but I wouldn't tell him that. I'm not sure I'd have a chance to tell him even if I wanted to, because I'm not positive he'll call me again.

"What the hell does that mean?"

I shrug even though she can't see me do it. "I don't know. We've seen each other once since that night at the Cowboy."

"Men are dumb," she mumbles. "Be patient with him, but not too patient."

"What's that mean? How can I be patient but not too patient?"

There's rustling on the other end of the phone. "What are you doing right now?"

"Sitting on the couch, contemplating the rest of my life."

"Why don't you meet me for lunch? My treat. Bear's working and I'm hungry. I hate dining alone."

I look around, knowing there's not much else except old pizza and ramen noodles in my kitchen. "Sure. I'd love to have lunch with you." Lord knows I don't have many friends. Hell, I don't have any, for that matter. It's been ages since I've been out with someone to talk over a good meal and relax without any pressure.

"Where do you live? I'll swing by and grab you. No use in wasting gas in two cars."

"How about I pick you up?" I tell her because I have a thing about who I let drive me. I've had one too many nightmares about car accidents to get in the car with anyone, especially an older person who might not see very clearly.

"Perfect. I'll text you my address. Wear something cute," she says and hangs up.

I pull the phone away from my ear and stare at the black screen. "Wear something cute," I repeat to myself with my eyebrows drawn, completely confused. "What the…" My phone beeps, and her address appears on the screen.

Lucky for me, I'm already dressed cute. I have on a pair of black leggings with a spaghetti-strap tank top that is tight around my bust and flowy near my waist. My hair is tied back in a messy ponytail that trails down my back, ending near my strapless bra. The sandals I'm wearing are my favorite too. They're black and strappy, but the most comfortable things I've ever worn on my feet.

I punch Fran's address into the GPS app on my phone and am pleasantly surprised that she lives only ten minutes away. I grab my purse, checking my face for a split second before dashing out the door, excited to spend time with Fran.

If I could've picked my foster mom, she would've been exactly like Fran. I like her no-bullshit attitude, and I don't care if Stone thinks she's nosy; he doesn't realize what a blessing that can be. The alternative is what I lived with, and knowing you're unimportant isn't something that feels good.

As soon as I pull up in front of Fran's house, she opens her front door and motions for me to come inside. I peer out my windshield, soaking in the beauty of the house. I can see Fran living in something so pretty, but Bear doesn't fit at all. He is too rough around the edges, and the two images don't mesh inside my brain.

I climb out of my car and am instantly hit by the heat and humidity. If my hair had any straightness left, it is surely gone now.

"I'm so happy you're here," Fran says, holding out her arms before I make it up the walkway. "Give me a hug."

I embrace her without a second thought. "Thank you for inviting me out."

She sways from side to side, not letting me go. "Thank you for saying yes to this old lady."

"Your house is beautiful," I tell her as I pull away from her arms.

"Come in for a minute. I need to grab my purse and shoes." She turns and steps inside the house, and I follow.

My eyes instantly go upward to a giant chandelier in the entryway. I'm impressed with the modernity of the style. It's not something I would expect from someone of Fran's age. "Wow."

"Bear decorated it."

I glance down at her with my mouth hanging open. "Really?"

She nods with the kindest smile. "He loves decorating."

My brain's close to short-circuiting with that nugget of information. Bear looks like anything he'd decorate would be covered in oil and made of steel or cement. The chandelier over my head is beautifully delicate, made of brass, with over a dozen small lights.

"I'm ready to go, and I'm starving."

"Where do you want to go?"

"We're going to Maria's."

"Oh. Where's that? I've never seen it." But that's not surprising. I still don't know the area very well. There's so much in such a small space that it's hard to distinguish every local business.

Although this isn't a big city, it definitely has some similarities to Chicago. I think I could live here a lifetime and still not know everything that's around me.

Fran walks out the door with her purse tucked under her arm. "It's not far from here. The best food you'll ever eat."

"What's the cuisine?"

It didn't take me long to realize that this area of Florida is seriously lacking in great food options. That's the thing I miss the most from Chicago. The food was the best, and if you had a taste for something, you'd find it somewhere within a few miles' radius.

"Italian. I hope that's okay."

"Okay? It's the best," I tell her as I follow her outside,

waiting for her to lock the front door. "Italian has always been my favorite."

"Maria's serves the best Italian in town."

"Perfect." I rush in front of her to open the passenger door to my car, but she shoos me away. I back away with my hands up. "Sorry. I was trying to be nice."

"Babe, I'm old but not an invalid. I can open my own door. It's nice of you, but the only person who opens a car door for me is my husband."

My heart melts a little at that statement. I stare at her over the roof of my car. "He opens the door for you?"

She nods with the brightest smile. "Always. And you don't dare settle for less. Too many shitheads out here."

Fran slides into her seat as I get into mine. "Chivalry isn't dead, baby girl. You've just been dating the wrong men."

That isn't a lie. She probably doesn't know how right she is with that statement. Jeff never opened a door for me. He'd hit me with it first. "How long have you and Bear been together?" I ask, making conversation as I start up the car, but then I remember I have no clue where I'm going. I grab my phone, pulling up GPS.

"There's no need. I know the way."

I stash my phone back in my purse. "Lead the way."

"Go back to the main road," she tells me before I pull out of her driveway. "And we've been together as long as I can remember. Maybe it's because I don't want to remember a time before him."

"That's really sweet." And it is. I've never had grandparents to look up to and watch grow old together. Long-lasting relationships haven't been a part of my life. They're something I've seen on television shows and figured were made-up.

"Tell me about your life."

I shrug as I keep my eyes on the road. "Not much to tell, Fran. I'm a foster kid from Chicago. Pretty basic."

She reaches over, touching my arm. "That's sad, baby."

"It is what it is."

"You have anyone at all? Your foster family or anything?"

I shake my head, ignoring the sadness of my life as much as possible so my eyes don't fill with tears. "I've been on my own since I was eighteen."

"Not anymore, sweetie. You have me."

"I have you?" I ask, confused.

"No one should be alone, and I've never had a daughter. I'm going to take you under my wing a little. Is that okay?"

"Is it okay? Is it okay?" I repeat, each time raising my voice a little. "Oh my God, Fran. That's the nicest offer anyone's ever given me."

With each passing year, my yearning for a family has only grown bigger.

She pats my arm. "Good. Now, what's going on with Stone?" She points for me to turn. "Why isn't he wrapped around your little finger yet?"

"It's complicated."

"From what I saw at the Neon Cowboy, there's nothing complicated about it. I saw two young kids who had the spark and sizzle. A man doesn't look at a woman the way he looked at you unless he's falling—and falling hard and fast."

"Fran," I say softly, feeling the need to let her know what was really happening. "It wasn't how it looked."

"It's exactly how it looked. I saw two young, beautiful people who were a perfect match. Two young people who were attracted to each other but weren't honest with themselves."

"Stone rescued me from a bad situation that night, Fran. I didn't even know him an hour before that."

"Time is irrelevant when it comes to soul mates, baby."

I glance over at her. "We're not soul mates."

"How do you know?"

"I…" I can't finish the statement because I don't know what we are exactly. "I don't believe in soul mates."

She faces forward, squinting to make out the road signs. "Make the next right. And Bear's my soul mate. My life wouldn't have been complete without him."

"You two have something special."

She barks out a laugh. "The man chased me relentlessly. We were never supposed to be, but what's meant to happen…happens."

I turn where she told me. "Fran, this is a residential area. Are you sure there's a restaurant here?"

"A restaurant? No, sweetie. We're going to my sister-in-law's. She makes the best food. You'll have nothing better."

"Your sister-in-law's?" My palms instantly begin to sweat. "I can just drop you off."

"No. No. You're invited."

This is more than I bargained for, but my stomach is growling at the thought of a home-cooked meal. "I don't know."

"Stone's grandmother is excited to meet you."

A knot forms in my stomach. Stone's grandmother? Holy crap. My heart picks up the pace, working overtime. "Fran."

She laughs again. "Relax, Opal. Maria is amazing. You'll see," she says. "I promise you won't regret it."

I want to believe her, but I'm more nervous than I have been in a very long time. "She knows about me?"

"Baby, we all know about you."

Stone had said there weren't any secrets in his family, especially when it came to the women and Fran. "What do you know?"

"Everything."

Shit. I can't imagine what she, or Stone's grandmother, thinks. A broke-ass girl, hanging out with Stone within minutes of her boyfriend walking out on her.

"Damn," I mutter.

"Stone's a good kid. A bit of a dummy when it comes to relationships, but otherwise sweet."

"He's been nothing but great to me." I don't tell her

about the other night and the fact that we slept together. We've already overcomplicated a complicated situation.

"Of course. He's just like his daddy. Mike is one of the best. He treats Mia like she walks on water. Don't accept anything less than being treated like a princess. But Mike wasn't always so smart. He was stubborn, and Stone's a carbon copy of that man."

I barely hear what she's saying because I'm too busy having a mini freak-out about having lunch with not only Stone's aunt, but also his grandmother.

"Third driveway."

One. Two. Three. I turn, and my eyes widen as soon as they land on his grandmother's house. It's not even a house. That's too small of a word for the mansion that's at the end of a long drive lined with the most beautiful hibiscus bushes.

"I know it's a lot. My sister-in-law can be flashy sometimes, but she's a great woman. She must be in order to put up with my brother's bullshit."

I duck my head, staring up at the grand entrance to what would've looked like a royal palace to me as a kid.

"I know. I know. It's a bit gaudy, but it needs to be big. When you have damn near fifty people over for dinner every weekend, you need something this grotesque."

I blink. "Fifty people?" I whisper.

They're an entire tribe, and I don't even have one other person to call my own. I always knew I'd missed out on a lot, but I haven't let myself really understand how much different my life is from others.

"You'll meet them all, but not today."

"I don't think—" I start to say, but Fran opens the door to the car and starts to get out. "Well, okay, then," I say to myself as the door closes.

For a split second, I think about running. This is a lot in a short amount of time. But thankfully, Stone's truck isn't anywhere to be seen. I can get through a lunch with two old ladies. I'm sure they'll spend the entire time talking about the good old days and their medications.

The front door to the house opens as I climb out, and a beautiful woman with gray hair greets Fran, looking over her shoulder at me. "You did it," she says to Fran. "I should've never doubted you."

I didn't ask Fran how she got my phone number, but I guarantee it was from the autobody shop because I can't see Stone giving it out to anyone in his family.

Fran turns to me with the biggest smile, waving her hand in my direction. "Maria, this is Opal, Stone's girl."

I lift my hand, raising a finger. "I'm not Stone's girl," I say again. Fran knows this but keeps on pushing the issue.

"Sure, sugar," Fran says. "Whatever you say."

"Finally," Maria, Stone's grandmother, says, motioning for me to step closer. "I've heard a lot about you."

I'm sure she has, from everyone in the family except Stone. He wasn't lying when he said there're no secrets between his relatives.

"Hi, ma'am," I say, giving her a small wave before being enveloped in an all-consuming hug. "Well, okay." I can barely wheeze out the words because she's crushing me with all her might.

"What a beautiful girl," she says, but I don't know if she's talking to me or her sister-in-law. "I've been dying to meet you." She pulls back, giving my face a quick once-over.

Up close, she looks much younger, and her face is kind. She has a softness to her, almost a glow. I can see her surrounded by a ton of grandchildren, spoiling them rotten and giving them lots of love.

"You have?" My voice doesn't hide my surprise at her words.

She nods and smiles. "Everyone's told me about you, even Stone."

I feel my eyebrows rise as I jerk my head back slightly. "Really?"

She nods again. "He doesn't say much, but when he was talking about you last weekend, I couldn't help but listen."

"Well…I…" I have nothing. I'm too shocked to form a coherent thought.

"Come in. Come in. Lunch is almost ready."

"Great. I'm famished," Fran tells her, walking inside before Stone's grandmother releases her hold on me.

"I hope you brought an appetite, sweetheart. I don't know what you like to eat, so I made a little of everything."

"I'm not picky." I used to be when I was little, but that ended quickly when I entered the foster care system. The woman I lived with didn't care about the food being delicious as long as it was cheap.

Maria slings her arm around my shoulder and guides me into her house. If the outside was impressive, the inside is nothing short of awe-inspiring. The house is so clean, I'm scared to even touch anything. She must spend hours upon hours scrubbing every surface.

"Your home is lovely," I tell her, trying not to gawk at the expensive, custom-designed interior.

"Thank you. It's a little much sometimes, but I can't sell it. There are too many memories here now. Children. Grandchildren. Great-grandchildren."

"I imagine so," I tell her as my gaze moves around while we walk through to the kitchen.

I'm hit by so many smells, and my stomach gurgles, knowing what's about to come.

"So, Opal, Fran told me you're from Chicago."

"Yes, ma'am."

Maria stops walking and turns to face me. "Sweetie, you can call me anything else in the world, but not ma'am, please. You can call me Maria or even Grams."

"I call her bitch." Fran shrugs with a small laugh. "I wouldn't go that route, though."

Maria waves her hand at her sister-in-law and rolls her eyes. "She's a bad influence. Don't listen to her."

I'm jealous of their easiness with each other. I never had any other siblings and have no one I have history with. What would that even feel like? They have no idea what it's like to be as alone as I am. It would be impossible for them to fathom, much like it hurts my brain and my heart to think about their abundance of people.

"Can I help with something?" I ask Maria. She's going to a lot of trouble to make this lunch possible and feeding an absolute stranger.

"You cook?" she asks, looking at me like I'm an enigma.

I nod. "Self-taught, so I'm probably not very good, but I'm willing to learn."

Maria pulls me tight to her side. "I like your spunk and willingness. But today, I'll handle everything. You sit and relax."

"Okay," I say, tucking a lock of my hair that escaped my ponytail behind my ear, feeling a little useless and spoiled.

Fran pats the stool next to her at the kitchen island. "Sit. Sit. I'll grab some wine."

"Water is good for me," I tell her, knowing it's too damn early in the day for me to be drinking if I want to stay awake.

The front door opens, and their eyes move that way. Mine follow when I hear, "I'm here, Gram. What's wrong?"

Stone.

11

STONE

I stop dead as soon as I walk into the kitchen and my eyes land on Opal. She's white as a ghost, looking every bit as surprised as I am.

"I'm sorry," she says immediately.

"For what?" I ask, walking up to her as the two nosiest women in my life watch in rapt amusement. "I know they"—I pitch my finger in their direction—"did this."

Opal laughs. "They're something else."

"They're something," I mutter.

My grandma walks up to me and takes my arm. "Hi, baby," she says so gently, I almost forget she lied to me to get me over here.

I peer down at my small grandmother, but the gentleness of her smile makes any anger I felt melt away. It's her superpower she has over all of us. "Gram, I thought something was wrong. Like really, really wrong. I was ready to call an ambulance. You scared the living shit out of me."

She places her head on my bicep for a second as a form of a hug. "I'm not going out yet, Stone. We needed one more for lunch, and Fran and I thought you would be the perfect person."

"How do you need one more for lunch? I've never heard of such a thing."

"Odd numbers are bad luck," Aunt Fran says from her spot at the kitchen table.

I swing my gaze her way, giving her a raised eyebrow. "You two are always up to something."

Aunt Fran laughs. "Lunch with three beautiful women isn't such a bad way to spend an afternoon."

My grandmother moves back to the stove as I take a step closer to Opal. She stares up at me, holding her breath, not moving a single muscle. I want her to be at ease. Being in a house with my aunt and grandma has to have her on edge.

I bend my neck as I reach for her face, cupping her cheek. "I'm glad you're here," I whisper against her skin before I place my lips ever so lightly on her cheek.

"You are?" she whispers, looking more than surprised.

I nod, staring into her blue eyes. "I was going to call you today, but this is way better."

"Why don't you kids sit, and we'll serve you," Grandma says as she stirs something on the stove.

"What's this we?" Aunt Fran asks from her comfortable chair.

"Get your ass up, Fran. Let the kids have a moment without you listening to their every word."

"I can hear them from there too, Mar."

"Fran," Grandma warns, and Fran scrambles to her feet but not without grumbling a few curse words under her breath.

I haven't let go of Opal's face, and I can't seem to make myself either. "How did they get you here?"

"Fran called."

"Fuckin' Tamara," I mutter, shaking my head, finally dropping my hand. "I'm sorry my cousin gave out your number."

Opal smiles, and the sight of her happy face makes my heart pick up a few paces. "It's okay. I like Fran."

"Damn right," Fran mumbles from the kitchen island.

"You're asking for trouble," I tell her, smiling back at this woman who hasn't left my mind since the day she walked into the shop.

Opal blushes and looks at my aunt and grandma. "You're really lucky, Stone."

"I guess I am, baby."

"Okay, kids. Take a seat."

I close my eyes and take a deep breath, readying myself for what's about to come.

"It's okay," Opal reassures me, brushing her fingertips against the bare skin of my forearm. "Relax, big guy."

"Don't be so dramatic. You're just like your daddy," Aunt Fran says, carrying a bowl of pasta to the table. "It's only lunch with two old ladies—and one really young and beautiful one, too."

"It's not like we called the priest to have you married

off before dessert," Gram adds.

Opal giggles, and the sound is so glorious my cock instantly jumps to life.

Bad timing, buddy.

Ain't shit going to happen right now. My gram and Aunt Fran, the world's two biggest boner killers, will make sure of that.

"You two sit by each other," Gram says, knowing well I can't and won't argue with her.

I pull out a chair for Opal, and she gracefully slides into place. "Thank you," she whispers.

I give her a chin lift before sitting down next to her. "You sure this is okay?" I ask her.

"It's great," she tells me with a nervous smile.

I'm sure lunch with two virtual strangers is anything but great for her. We watch as Aunt Fran and Gram carry bowl after bowl and plate after plate to the table.

"Who can eat all this food?" I touch my silverware, trying to stop myself from touching Opal. "This is a feast. Not a lunch."

Gram glares at me. "Hush."

"Do you always eat like this for lunch?" Opal asks my gram.

"No, sweetheart. This is a special occasion."

Oh boy. Here we go. The two old birds are colluding with each other, trying to bring us together.

"And what's the special occasion?" I ask, challenging my grandmother's statement.

"It's Fran's birthday."

I stare at her, knowing damn well Fran's birthday is not even in this month. If I were alone, I'd call bullshit, but I'll let her have this one...for now.

"Oh. Happy birthday, Fran. Do you and Bear have something fun planned for tonight?" Opal asks my aunt.

Fran smirks. "Child, you don't even want to know what we have planned for tonight."

I almost choke on the water I decided to sip at the wrong moment. "Aunt Fran," I cough out, pounding on my chest.

Opal laughs. "Oh wow. You lucky woman." She winks at Fran.

If I could crawl under the table and die, I would. I don't want any images of Bear and Fran having sex running through my mind in any capacity.

"Bear's a beast," Fran adds.

The water threatens to come back up, but somehow, I keep it down. "Stop," I tell Fran. "It's too much."

Fran gawks at me from the other side of the table. "Stone, someday you're going to get old, and if you're lucky, your parts will still work too."

Fuck me. "My parts will always work."

Gram and Fran laugh in unison.

"That's precious," Gram says, patting my hand. "Age has a way of giving everything a mind of its own."

"So, Opal," Fran says, and nothing that comes out of her mouth that starts with "so" is ever good. It's her opening line to being nosy. "How's work going? What do you do again?"

Opal's shoulders sag forward. "I lost my job a few days ago."

"Oh dear," Gram says.

"What are you going to do now?" Fran asks.

Gram holds up the bowl of pasta to me, and I take it from her, letting the women talk while I listen. It's a skill my dad and uncles taught me at an early age.

Opal shrugs one shoulder. "I put in a few applications."

"What do you do?" Fran asks again.

"Commercial graphic design, specifically social media campaigns."

"That sounds fancy," Fran says. "I don't know anything about social media. I can barely make a phone call, let alone anything else."

Opal smiles at my aunt. "I love the sense of community it gives people."

"Are there many openings around here?"

Opal's smile vanishes. "Not like there were in Chicago. There're a few, but the pay is low."

"It's always best to be your own boss. Why don't you freelance? Or start your own company?" Gram asks Opal, sounding way more with the times than I thought possible.

"I thought about it," Opal tells my grandmother as she's handed a plate of chicken cutlets. "I don't know many people around here, though."

"We know everyone," Gram tells her. "We have a few charity organizations we're involved with, and maybe you can help us grow those bigger. I'll talk to a couple of my friends and see what we can do and what we need."

Opal sits a little straighter. "You'd do that?"

Gram nods with a small smile. "Of course, sweetheart. Everyone deserves a chance to do what they love. Wait, doesn't Tamara do something with this stuff?"

I love that my gram calls it stuff like it's something she can't quite comprehend.

"She does," I answer. "She does social media marketing."

"Get those two in touch," Gram tells me.

"I will, but they've already met."

Opal fidgets with her silverware, unsure of what to say.

"I bet ALFA could use some too. It doesn't hurt to drive more business their way," Fran says.

"What's ALFA?" Opal asks.

"It's pronounced like alpha, but the guys like the spelling A-L-F-A better, for whatever reason. It's a security company, and they also deal with private investigations and whatever other shenanigans they can get into. Stone's uncles own it, and Bear works there, along with my son, Morgan," Fran explains.

Opal moves the cutlet around on her plate to make room for more food. "That's too nice. You don't need to do all this."

They're not doing it only out of the kindness of their hearts; they're trying to make her more of a permanent fixture in our lives. They know I like her and are making it damn near impossible for me to walk away from whatever is happening between us.

Gram holds out another plate to Opal that's filled with

marinated and grilled eggplant. "It'll help get you started. Having a few clients will lend you more credibility in town. There are a lot of small businesses, and I bet many of them have no idea how to market to the people around here, especially the new residents."

Opal stares at my gram with her mouth hanging open. "I don't know if they'd take a chance on me. I'm new and have no experience on my own."

Fran reaches over and touches Opal's arm, giving her a sugary smile. "Babe, you need to change that attitude around. You're the shit. Remember that. People will see you as you see yourself. Look at Stone."

I'm about to stuff my mouth with a giant piece of chicken cutlet when I stop with my fork in midair. "What did I do?"

"You think you're the shit, don't you?" Fran asks, eyeing me with her head tilted to one side.

"I *am* the shit, Auntie," I tell her with so much confidence in my tone. I know what I am and what I bring to the table.

"See?" Fran waves her hand in my direction. "You feel it coming off him, don't you?" she asks Opal. "His confidence."

Opal gazes at me and nods. "I do. I like that about him."

"People like that about other people. The business owners won't know what you don't know. They'll be drawn to your confidence. You need to repeat to yourself, *I am the shit*."

Opal laughs, shaking her head at the weird pep talk my aunt is giving her. "I don't think it's so easy."

"It is. Put on a good push-up bra, some lipstick and mascara, and go slay all the business owners."

"She doesn't need all that stuff," I grumble, thinking about her looking more beautiful with her tits all pushed out. I would rip any man's eyes out for looking at her the wrong way or their arms off for trying anything funny.

"Hush up," Fran chides me like I'm a small child. "She's got to play the game."

I shake my head, grinding my teeth. "No games and no push-up bra."

Gram bites her lip to hold in her laugh. "Men are ridiculous."

"They are," I agree with her. "It shouldn't take a pair of tits to get business. Maybe that's how things worked in the olden days, but they don't work that way anymore."

"Do you have a portfolio?" Gram asks her.

"I do. It's small, but I could go through and build it up a bit. Give it a little pizzazz."

"Do that," Gram says, pointing her fork in Opal's direction. "Once you're done, we'll make sure to introduce you to everyone we know. But until then, I'll talk to my closest friends and family."

"I'll talk to the ladies at the shop. See what we can do. I think the ladies were talking about trying to figure out an advertising campaign, but they don't have much extra time."

"See?" Gram ticks her chin in my direction. "There's

your first client."

"Maybe," Opal says softly, moving the food around on her plate.

"It's a lock, babe," I tell her, knowing damn well I'll move heaven and earth to make it happen. "We'll be your first client." And if I had my way, we'd be her only one, but I know that isn't possible.

"Good. That's settled." Gram smiles. "Now, what's going on with you two?" she asks point-blank.

I jerk backward, shocked by her directness. Gram usually isn't as in your face about relationships, but here she is, being nosy as hell. I'd expect that type of question out of my aunt Fran, but not Gram.

Opal looks at me out of the corner of her eye, and I do what any sane person would do. I answer for us both. "We're friends. Good friends."

"It doesn't hurt to have close friends, but when you get to my age, you know a thing or two about a thing or two. And from what I'm seeing, there's a lot more than friendship and chicken cutlets sizzling in this room."

"You two would make beautiful children," Fran adds, causing me to choke on a mouthful of pasta.

"I can see them now," Gram says. "I'm not getting any younger, you know."

I pound on my chest, trying to get the food that's scraping the insides to go down my throat. "I'm fully aware," I get out between coughs. "Give us a little time. We just met, for Christ's sake."

Gram shrugs her shoulders. "Time is a made-up thing,

Stone. You can't grasp it, and no matter what you do, there's never enough of it. Take it from two old birds."

Fran rolls her eyes. "Who's the second old bird, Maria? I'm not old. Maybe you are, but I'm still a young thing."

I turn my head, taking in Opal's profile. She's staring at my aunt and grandmother, slowly eating small morsels of food. "I'm sorry for them."

She gazes at me over her shoulder, almost stealing my breath with the softness of her features. "I like them. Don't apologize."

She only likes them because she doesn't know how much bullshit these two can get into. If there's trouble, they're right there, fanning the flames.

"They're sweet."

I bark out a laugh. "They're not as sweet as you think."

Opal touches my hand, sending a scattering of shock waves through my system. "You're lucky, Stone. They love you enough to ask questions even if they're uncomfortable."

"See?" Aunt Fran says, waving her knife around the table. "She's a smart woman. You men don't know how lucky you are to have such caring women in your lives."

I grumble under my breath but try to stay positive because I know Opal hasn't had anyone give a damn about her in years. "I know. I know," I say, lifting my hands up. "I'm the luckiest son of a bitch."

"You're having a damn good lunch with three beautiful women. What could be better?" Fran asks me.

I could think of a dozen things, and they all involve

Opal being naked.

"Do you have anyone else around here, sweetie?" Gram asks Opal.

Opal shakes her head.

"You have us now. We have dinner on Sunday, every Sunday. You're always welcome in our home."

"That's nice," Opal says, squirming in her chair a little. "I couldn't impose."

"Don't be silly. We feed a small army every weekend, and one more mouth is no imposition. No one should be alone in this world, especially when we have so much to give."

Fuck. I'm not mad about them inviting Opal. I'm pissed at myself for being such a pansy about getting more involved with her. Not only does my family have a lot to offer, but so do I. I have no idea what it's like for her to be utterly and completely alone, and I'm letting my fear of something that could very well be damn near amazing get in the way.

"You should come," I tell Opal, pushing aside my stupid fear. "You already know most of my cousins. They'd love to have another girl here."

Opal dips her chin and blinks. "You'd want me here?"

I smile at her, wishing I could pull her against me and stare into her deep blue eyes. "I want you everywhere," I admit for the first time ever, forgetting for a split second that my grandma and aunt are sitting with us.

"Stone," Opal whispers, giving the two nosy onlookers a side-eye as her face turns pink.

"Come, Opal. If you hate it, you don't have to come again. I want you there."

Opal rubs her hands down her pants, looking like she's about to curl into herself. "Are you sure?"

I nod. "Never been more sure about anything in my life," I lie, shaking my leg underneath the table and trying not to hyperventilate.

"Perfect," Gram says with a clap. "You can meet everyone at once."

"Way to give her anxiety," I tell Gram, keeping my eyes trained on Opal. "It'll be okay."

She nods. "I'd love it," she says softly. "Thank you, Maria."

"You know," Gram says, and I brace myself because whatever is about to come out of her mouth is going to send me into a tailspin. She never starts anything with "you know" unless it's going to be big. "If you two work out, you're going to have to call me Gram, too."

Opal's smile falls. "I've never had a grandmother."

Her words are like a dagger to my heart. I can't imagine never having a grandma. Hell, I have two. They can be a pain in the ass sometimes, but they're filled with love. My life would be so boring if I didn't have them to spoil me like they've done since the day I was born.

I didn't know much when I was younger, but I always knew I was loved. There has never been a day when I haven't felt that energy around me. And until I met Opal, I didn't know there were people out there who didn't know what that felt like.

"That's tragic, sweetie," Fran whispers. "I'll be your grandma, no matter what happens. You and Stone don't work out, I'll be your Granny Fran."

Opal's gaze swings Fran's way. "You'd do that?"

Fran smiles with a quick nod. "I can never have too many grandchildren, and I'd be honored to have one as great as you."

"You don't know what you're getting into," I warn Opal, but I also know Fran is one of the best. She loves to cause trouble, but she's a ball of fun and love.

"Zip it, buddy," Fran says to me, pointing her damn knife my way.

"You pick this old bird up every once in a while for lunch and shopping, and you've got yourself a granny."

"Bear ready for another grandkid?" I ask her, risking my life and limb with my dumb question.

"Yep. The man is ready for anything I throw his way, even a kid. And hell, he doesn't even have to change a diaper this time."

"You guys are too much," Opal says, her blue eyes glistening in the sunlight streaming through the windows.

Shit. She's tearing up. I'm so wrapped up in my fear that I've pushed aside the way she must be feeling. I want to swoop in and rescue her. I want to give her all the things she was never given. And in this moment, I know my fear is inconsequential in comparison to my need to see her happy.

There is nothing better than a smiling Opal, and I'll do everything in my power to keep that smile on her face.

12

OPAL

It's Friday afternoon, and I've been summoned to Nuts & Bolts by Tamara. There's no doubt in my mind Fran and Maria have been chewing her ear off about me and twisting her arm to find me work.

They're nice old women. Stone told me they were nosy, but that is an understatement. Though they mean well.

"Hey." Tamara hops off her counter-height stool as soon as I walk through the customer entrance.

I push my cheap plastic sunglasses on top of my head. "Hey. Thanks for this." I give her a smile, trying to hide my apprehension about the whole thing. "I wasn't expecting you to call so soon."

Tamara comes around the counter to stand in front of me. She's simply stunning. A natural beauty with a definite wild side. Her ripped jeans and classic rock T-shirt round out the look perfectly. "Are you kidding me? I've been dying to get you alone."

"Oh," I mumble, unable to stop my eyebrows from rising in surprise. "Well, here I am." I glance around, noticing there's no one except us in the customer waiting room.

She reaches out and takes my hand, leading me to the chairs. "So, first things first." She gently pushes my arm to place me in a seat before she takes the one next to me. "Gram called to tell me about the bind you're in and that you're a graphic designer. Did she get that right?"

I nod. "It's what I used to do in Chicago. I worked for a big advertising company."

"That would be so damn cool."

"It was," I tell her with a half-smile, wanting to kick myself for giving up such an amazing job for such a loser like Jeff.

I have tried for the last month not to beat myself up on a daily basis for making such a stupendous mistake. Some days I fail, but I'm getting better at only looking forward instead of dwelling on the past.

"I started my own local marketing company right after college. Nuts & Bolts was my first client." She glances around the room, beaming with pride. "I can't take all the credit for what this place has become, but I had a heavy hand in its success."

I love that she isn't shy when it comes to talking about her accomplishments and her abilities. "Is that how you met your husband?" I ask her.

She turns her gaze back to me with a smirk. "No, babe. I met him before I finished college. It's one of the perks when you sleep with the owner of the company...you get their work without any questions."

"I imagine so," I say with a hint of laughter in my voice. She's not bashful, and I love this about her.

It's something I've noticed with all of Stone's female relatives. They're strong women who take no bullshit, but they sure as hell give a lot of it.

"He was my first client, but the business has grown by leaps and bounds. I have too much now to keep up with it and help here at the garage. Then there's my kids and family." She grabs her head, placing her thumb and middle fingers on her temples. "It's enough to give me a headache or eventually a heavy dose of burnout."

"I'm sorry."

She drops her hand away from her face and waves off my words. "It could be worse, right?"

"Yeah," I whisper, knowing my life definitely falls into the worse category when compared to hers. "For sure."

"I usually don't work here at the garage anymore, but Old Man Pete has been out for a few weeks. He had a death in the family and had to go back up north to deal with some family affairs."

I cover my mouth with my hand. "That's awful."

"It is." Her shoulders sag forward. "I hate this for him. He's the nicest old man ever, and he does a great job here at the garage. He keeps all those meatheads in line and knows everything there is to know about cars."

"That's useful."

She nods. "Anyway, I was already behind on my own business before Pete left, but now, I'm even further behind and drowning a little more every day. Maybe you can bring your portfolio to my grandparents' house on Sunday, and I'll look it over. If I like what I see, you can start work on Monday morning."

"Really?" I ask, unable to hide the astonishment in my voice. "That soon?"

She nods enthusiastically. "Fuck yeah. I'd hire you this minute, but I wouldn't even have the time to go over everything with you today. Pete will be back soon, and then I can concentrate on my own shit."

"I wasn't planning on going to your grandparents' house," I admit without looking her in the eye. "I feel funny."

"Fuck that," she snaps. "Don't feel funny. It's like a goddamn circus some Sundays, but don't let that frighten you. You'll blend in, and you've already met seventy-five percent of the people who will be there anyway."

"I don't know, Tamara. I didn't feel like Stone was entirely comfortable with me coming."

She grunts and reaches into her back pocket, fishing out her phone.

"What are you doing?" I ask her as she starts to tap on the screen.

"Nothing," she mumbles, pressing away.

I lean forward to try to see what she's doing, but she bends backward, making it impossible.

There's one ring and then a *hello.*

"Stone."

Fuck me.

No. No. No.

I want to crawl under something and hide, but there's only a giant stone coffee table that's made out of a literal boulder and then the chairs around the room that leave no room to slide underneath.

Shit.

"What's up, T?" he says, sounding like he was asleep.

Tamara holds up a finger to her lips as she stares at me. "Do you want Opal to come to dinner on Sunday? What do you think about Gram inviting her?"

There's rustling on his end. "Yeah, T. I want her there. I'm glad Gram invited her because I probably would've been too chickenshit. I like the girl. Like her way more than I probably fucking should, which is fucking nuts. I can't get her out of my damn mind. Do you have any idea what that's like?"

Tamara's smiling at me, and I do my best to ignore the way my stomach's doing backflips.

Stone likes me.

More than that...he can't get me out of his mind.

The feeling is entirely mutual, and that scares the ever-living shit out of me.

"I do, babe. Happened with me and Mammoth. He wasn't in my plans, but when we met, there was no escaping the pull he had over me. It was some fucked-up, crazy-ass shit."

"You meetin' with her today?" he asks.

"Yep."

"You going to hire her?"

"I think so. If her portfolio is solid."

"Do me a favor, T. Give her a chance. I need her to stick around for a while, and right now, there isn't much keeping her here."

I want to tell him that is a lie. I have him. He makes me want to stick around. In all honesty, I don't have anywhere else to be. I don't have family in other parts of the country. I have nothing except the here and now…and Stone.

"You got it, buddy. Anything for you. But you're going to owe me big-time for this, got it?"

He sighs. "Whatever you want, T. Anything at all. You name it, it's yours."

"I could use a babysitter at the end of this month so that Mammoth and I can go away for a night to get some alone time, if you know what I mean."

"I know what you mean, but I don't want to, cousin. Yeah. Yeah. Fine. I'll watch the rug rats for a night. How bad could they be?"

Tamara snickers. "They're angels," she tells him, shaking her head at me. "Time will fly by."

"Whatever. I always have a special Benadryl cocktail if they start to act up."

"You wouldn't," she says.

"I'm fucking kidding. Those babies love me. I'm the fun one in the family."

"You're going to find out what happens when you give

them all that candy you like to make rain down on them when you're around. You're going to have a really awesome experience. Anyway, I got to run. Opal's here to talk."

"Fuck. Okay. Don't tell her about this conversation. Got me?"

"Loud and fucking clear, babysitter."

"You're an asshole," he grumbles before ending the call.

"See, he wants you there. It's settled."

"You sure it won't be weird?" I ask her, wiping my hands down the front of my jeans, still feeling uneasy about the entire thing.

"I promise. Would I lie?" she asks, after I just listened to her lie her ass off to her own cousin and rope him into doing something he didn't have to do.

I stare at her without saying a word.

"Yeah. I know. But he deserves this type of shit. Trust me. You can ask any of the other cousins. I may have to set up a camera or two inside the house to watch him cry when the kids are running around the house with the zoomies at two in the morning because he stuffed them full of chocolate and ice cream."

I snicker, picturing him losing his mind. "He'll have a breakdown."

"I know," she says with a laugh. "I'm banking on that."

"You trust him enough to leave your kids with him."

"Yeah, babe. Stone is solid. He can be a douchebag, but that's only because he has a penis, which somehow short-circuits his brain. But otherwise, he's a great person."

"That's nice," I reply, unsure of what else to say.

"Now, what's going on with the two of you?"

I shrug. "I don't know."

"I know you two slept together."

My eyes widen. "You do?"

She nods. "Yep. Don't be ashamed. Sex is part of being alive. But I've never heard my cousin talk about anyone the way he talks about you. I'm wondering if the feeling is mutual, or if you're too scared to tell him that you're just not that into him. So, which is it? You like him or want to kick his muscly ass to the curb?"

"I like him," I admit without hesitation. "I like him a lot."

I don't know why it sounds so weird coming out of my mouth, but it does. It sounds almost juvenile, but the words fit. I'm leery of getting involved with someone else so soon after Jeff, but Stone is the one who saved me from him in the first place. It's been a month already anyway. I mean, is there an acceptable period of time to wait between relationships that end the way ours did? It's not like the guy was nice to me. I wasn't mourning the end of us in any way, shape, or form.

Tamara claps her hands. "Perfect."

"It is?"

"Oh, girl. It's fan-freaking-tastic. I've been waiting what feels like forever for my cousin to settle down."

I almost choke on my own spit. "Settle down?" My

voice cracks when I say the words. "I didn't say anything about settling down."

She pats my leg. "I have this sixth sense about these things. Trust me on this. A man like Stone doesn't talk about a woman the way he talks about you unless your future is in the back of his mind, wearing that white dress and promising him forever."

"I don't know if—"

She shakes her head at me. "Trust me. Just ride it out." Movement in the garage catches her eye. "It's worth it."

I follow her gaze, seeing her husband. They go together perfectly. Both beautiful. Both wild. I'd almost say they were made for each other.

"How did you two meet, if you don't mind my asking?"

She doesn't look my way as a smile spreads across her face. "I went to meet another guy but ended up in Mammoth's bed."

"How's that work?" I ask in amazement as I stare at her hunk of a man. You'd have to be dead not to appreciate his rugged handsomeness.

She sighs, resting her elbow on her knee and chin in her palm. "It's a long story." She smirks to herself. "It was wild, though, and I never looked back or regretted a minute of my time with him."

"That's sweet," I say softly, a little jealous of their relationship.

"My family wasn't thrilled about us as a couple, but they realized in short order that we were the real deal."

"Why weren't they happy?" I'm being nosy, but since I've met her family, I don't think it will feel like prying to her because it is their norm.

She blinks a few times before giving her attention back to me. "He was in an MC."

"MC?"

"Motorcycle club."

My eyes widen, but I shouldn't be surprised. He looks like he was born to ride. "Really?"

She nods. "Dangerous shit, but he got out. He chose me and our life over that one."

"Smart man."

"Magic pussy," she responds without missing a beat.

"What?"

"Nothing, doll," she says and pats my leg again. "Just mumbling bullshit."

"Oh. Okay."

I have a feeling I'll hear more about this at a later date, so I don't dare push. She's already told me enough, probably more than I would've told someone in her position.

"Can you be here on Monday at nine? Pete needs a few more days."

"Don't you want to see my portfolio first?"

"Of course, but I know I'm going to love it, and anyway, I really need the help. I'm sure you'll be able to slide right in and take a ton off my plate."

"Nine works," I tell her, dropping any argument. She's offering me a job, and I'm being an idiot by trying to talk her out of it.

"We'll talk about pay when I see your work. If you change your mind then, no harm, no foul."

"Okay," I say, sitting up a little straighter, trying to contain my excitement about finally landing a job in my field. "Am I allowed to freelance with other customers and companies?"

"Of course. Don't be silly. Get all the work you can while you can."

"Thanks, Tamara. I don't know how I'll ever thank you."

"Don't mention it, Opal. Just give my bonehead cousin a shot, and we'll call it even."

I can do that. I was already going to give him a shot. He's been nicer to me than anyone else has been in almost a decade.

So far, I don't know what I like more, Stone or his family, but I know I want to be part of them in any way possible. I'll do whatever I can to make it possible, and if there is a white picket fence and wedding bells in the future, I'll be a-fucking-okay with that too.

13

STONE

"I'M SO NERVOUS." OPAL RUNS HER PALMS UP AND DOWN the thighs of her jeans. "Am I being ridiculous?" she asks, glancing in my direction. "I feel like I want to jump out of my skin." I've convinced her to leave her portfolio in the car until later. She's worried enough about meeting my family without adding that right away.

I stare at her, soaking in her beauty. "Do you want to leave? I'll take you anywhere you want to go."

I'd have a lot of explaining to do to my family, but screw it. If Opal wants to go somewhere else, I'll go with her.

She turns her eyes back toward my grandparents' house. "No. I want to go, but…"

"I promise they'll be nice."

She smiles. "I'm sure they will be, but what if they don't like me?" The question is honest even if it's entirely ridiculous.

"They love everyone, and you'll be no different, but if you're not comfortable, we can ditch this place and head to the beach."

"Is it far?" she asks without taking her eyes off the front door.

"Is what far?"

"The beach."

My mouth falls open as I stare at her profile. "You've never been to the beach?"

She shakes her head. "I tried once. I thought it was a beach, but it was a weird little island with trees and cement."

"We're going to fix that. You want to go to the beach today? I love the beach."

She turns toward me. "Take me later," she says softly. "I want to watch the sunset."

"Prepare to be obsessed."

Her eyes soften. "Why are you so easy?"

I laugh because I know I'm a complicated clusterfuck. "I'm not easy at all." Unless we're talking about sex, then I'm the easiest person in the world. Everything else, I'm more than happy to be difficult. But there's something about Opal that makes me want to dive into the mundane. I'm easy for her, but no one else.

She sucks in a deep breath, rubbing her palms together, and closes her eyes. "I can do this."

I watch in fascination, wondering if she's about to have a full-blown panic attack. I reach out, placing my hand on her arm. "If you get overwhelmed, let me know, and we'll leave."

She opens her eyes, and she appears calmer than before. I'd like to think it's because of my hand on her, but that's my egotistical thinking. "I'm ready." She places her hand on the door handle.

I give her arm a squeeze, bringing her attention back to me. "They're going to love you," I reassure her, leaving out the bit about how I'm falling in love with her. If I feel that way about her, I know they're going to go bananas.

"Thank you," she says before pushing open the truck door.

I release my hold on her arm before opening my door and hopping out of the cab. "You've got this," I whisper to myself. "Don't be such a goddamn douchebag."

"What?" she asks as she rounds the front of the truck.

"Nothing," I tell her, feeling like a moron. "Just mumbling to myself."

"Is Fran here?" she asks, surveying all the cars and bikes in the front yard.

"Yep. She comes early to help Gram. Well…" I pause, remembering how inedible Fran's cooking is. "She comes to keep Gram company while she cooks, at least. Fran's cooking is shit."

Opal's eyebrows rise. "Really?"

I put my hand on Opal's lower back, guiding her through the maze of vehicles. "Yeah. Thank God Bear isn't a picky eater because the man would wither away to nothing."

Opal laughs as she walks, not pulling away from my touch. "Are you a good cook?"

"I cook a mean ramen."

"What else, or is that the extent of your culinary skills?"

"No. I can cook more, but it's just me and I'm too lazy to spend hours preparing food for only myself. How about you?"

"What I make is edible, but it's not like your grandma's food."

"No one's is like hers." I open the front door, and we're instantly met by loud voices.

"Are they fighting?" she asks, staring into the house like someone's going to jump out from behind a piece of furniture and attack her.

"They're only talking, which, more often than not, sounds like shouting. But I can promise, it's civil. I swear they're all going deaf, and every year it gets louder and louder."

Opal takes a step inside, and I follow her, my hand never leaving her back.

"We're here," I say to no one.

"They can't possibly hear you," Opal tells me.

But suddenly, Fran appears and is heading right toward us. "Finally," she says, holding out her arms to Opal. "Gimme a hug."

Opal doesn't immediately open her arms. She looks almost overwhelmed by the warmth of Fran, and if I'm honest, I'm a little shocked myself.

Fran has always been kind, but there's a whole lot of saltiness to her too. But not when it comes to Opal. Fran's embraced her, wanting her to be part of her family, or our family in general. Maybe it's the Chicago connection that's pulled Fran in, but whatever it is, I don't question it.

"Are you okay?" Fran asks Opal as she wraps her arms around her, holding her as if they've known each other their entire lives.

"I am now," Opal says, melting into Fran's arms.

Fran peers up at me with the warmest smile as she keeps hugging Opal. "Everyone's excited to meet you."

Opal pulls away slightly, gazing at Fran. "I hope I don't disappoint them."

Fran takes a step back, finally separating from my girl. "Baby, you could never disappoint us. This is a no-judgment zone. This is a house and family built on love and acceptance. Remember that as you walk around today and meet everyone."

"This is really overwhelming."

"Just wave and smile, then you can go out back and hang out with the kids. You don't even need to say anything if you don't want to."

"Oh, okay," Opal says, looking a little more relaxed.

"Let Stone do all the talking. He's always got a lot to say."

"Auntie." I shake my head. "I'm not *that* talkative."

"No. No, you aren't, but you could be when you need to rescue your girl."

I place my hand back at the small of her back, wanting nothing more than to touch her. "I'll take care of her."

Fran waves us in. "Come on. Let's meet everyone."

Opal peers over her shoulder at me with a slightly terrified smile. "Don't leave me," she pleads.

"I'd never. You're stuck with me."

I fully expect the entire family to come stalking toward us to get a good look at Opal. I'm sure they're intrigued by her since I've never brought anyone to Sunday dinner with me. But to my surprise, when we step into the back of the house, they all remain seated.

The older people are all inside, lounging between the kitchen and the living room.

"She's here," Fran announces, waving her hand in Opal's direction.

There's a deafening silence.

Opal waves, jostling her weight back and forth from one foot to the other. "Hi," Opal says.

Fran slides her hand around Opal's arm, linking herself to her. "You met Bear."

Bear nods, giving Opal the biggest smile. "Good to see you again."

"And Maria."

"Hi," Opal says softly, giving my grams a giant and genuine smile.

"I hope you're hungry, sweetheart. Make yourself at home."

"Thank you, Maria."

"These are Stone's parents, Mia and Mike."

My mom and dad get up, and I brace myself for whatever nonsense is about to come.

Opal's eyes lock on my dad as her neck cranes back to look up at his face. "Sweet Jesus," Opal mutters. "You're a..." She snaps her mouth shut. "Shit, did I say that out loud?"

My dad laughs, looking like a giant in front of Opal. "I get that a lot."

Ma smacks my dad with the back of her hand square in the middle of his chest. "No, he doesn't. Hi, Opal. I'm Mia. It's so nice to finally meet you. My son has told me a lot about you."

Opal peers back at me. "You talk about me?"

My face heats and I want to pull my mom to the side and tell her not to embarrass me, but I know there's no use. It wouldn't be a day if they didn't do their best to shower me with their love and act a fool. "A little," I admit, which is a lie because I've talked more about her to my parents than I have about anyone else in the world.

"If he acts up, let me know. I'll deal with him," Dad tells Opal.

"He's been nothing short of a complete gentleman."

My father stares at me, looking shocked and impressed. "I taught him everything he knows."

My mom rolls her eyes. "Babe, don't lie. You're two steps above caveman. If he's being nice, that's all me."

My dad grabs my mom around the waist and hauls her backward into him. His arms seal around her body as he tucks his face into her neck. "He's the best of both of us, baby girl."

"I'm sorry about them," I tell Opal, trying not to get sick over their public display of affection. They've been like this my entire life, and I imagine they always will be for as long as they're both alive.

Opal doesn't take her eyes off them and their ogling of each other. "It's sweet."

"Don't hog the girl," Aunt Max says from the back of the room. "Give her space. We all want a good look at the one who caught Stone's eye."

Opal blushes but doesn't look like she's about to run.

"Come on," I tell Opal, pulling her away from my parents.

I spend the next fifteen minutes introducing Opal to the older generation. They keep their questions short and not too intrusive, which isn't like them at all. I'm guessing they had a conversation about her past and current situation before we arrived. Fran probably filled everyone in on everything.

"They're all yours?" Opal asks me, staring over the group of my aunts and uncles.

"This is only a small portion of them."

"So fucking lucky," she whispers.

My grandpa comes strolling into the kitchen from the hallway. "Sorry about that. Harley and Jackson wanted to go for a walk to try to catch some butterflies."

"Did you get any?" Gram asks him.

"No. They tried like hell, though." His eyes find me in

the crowd and then move to Opal. "Hi, sweetheart. I'm this big lug's grandpa, Sal."

"Hi, Grandpa Sal."

Those words instantly make my gramps' face light up. "Sweet and beautiful." He reaches for her hand, lifting it to his lips. "It's a pleasure to finally meet you."

"You too," she says, instantly drawn into my grandpa's charm. "Thank you for having me over for dinner."

"The more, the merrier," he tells her, releasing her hand. "Make yourself comfortable, and don't leave hungry. Try to keep that one in line." His eyes flicker to me. "He can be a pistol."

Opal chuckles. "He can be something else."

"You have no idea, but if you want stories, I have enough on him that you could blackmail him for decades."

Opal's chuckle grows louder, and my stomach flutters. The sound is so beautiful, and I hate myself for feeling that way. I've turned into a mushy fool around her, and if I could, I'd punch myself square in the face to snap the fuck out of it.

I'm starting to not even recognize myself. I used to care about me and only me. But ever since Opal dropped into my life, I'm more concerned with her happiness than my own.

"I may just take you up on that offer," Opal replies.

My grandpa steps away and heads toward my grandma. He's quick to give her a kiss on the cheek and pat her butt. "You need me?" he asks her as Opal watches them.

"Always, Sal, but not right now. Behave," she warns him.

"They're cute," Opal says from beside me. "I wonder what that's like?"

I place my arm around her waist, holding her a little closer to me. "What what's like?"

"Loving someone for that long," she whispers.

"I have no idea," I mutter, wondering if I'll ever have that in my life.

My grandparents were already married at my age. Probably a kid or two in tow, too. I can't imagine living that life, but I know I want what they have when I'm older, but I'm not ready for it now—or at least, I thought I wasn't.

"Everyone is so happy and loving," Opal tells me, resting her head on my arm, finally relaxed.

"That they are."

"Fucking lucky," she mumbles. "You have no idea, Stone."

I want to argue because I know I hit the freaking jackpot, but no matter what I say, it won't sound genuine. I can only assume what the opposite feels like. I'll never understand what it's like to be alone. I haven't had a minute's peace my entire life.

I squeeze her side and enjoy the moment, looking around at my family through her eyes, with Opal relaxed against me like we've been this way forever. It feels so natural and like she was meant to be here with me in this very moment.

When did I turn into a freaking Hallmark card? I want to run to the bathroom and check my balls to make sure they're still there. Never in my life have I talked such pure and absolute flowery shit, and I am scaring myself a little.

What the hell is going on with me?

You're falling for her, you big dummy.

I swallow, pushing all thoughts of love right out of my mind. I'm not ready. I'm not sure when I ever will be. I want Opal, but can I imagine taking the next step?

Fuck.

"Want to go outside?" I ask her, knowing my cousins will be more chill instead of filling her mind and mine with all the lovey-dovey bullshit.

"Yeah. I could use a breather," she says, but she has no idea that she isn't going to get any respite outside either.

My cousins may not hang all over each other, but quiet, they are not. They're going to have more questions than anyone because they don't have a limit to their nosiness.

The sliding glass door opens, and Tamara pops her head into the kitchen. "You bitches coming outside or what?" she asks, staring right at us but with a smile.

"We're coming," I tell Tamara, glaring.

Way to play it cool, cousin.

"Well, get your fine asses out here. We have two cold beers waiting for you."

"Thank God," Opal breathes, moving toward the sliding glass door without hesitation, straight from the frying pan into the fire.

14

OPAL

I let my eyes wander around the large table. Stone's cousins are each fantastic in their own way and completely different. None of them has the same personality besides being outgoing and friendly.

They've made me feel welcome although I'm a virtual stranger. If I had any reservations about coming, they vanished long ago.

Stone leans over to whisper in my ear. "What's wrong?"

I shrug. There are so many emotions running through me at the same time. I turn my head so our mouths are almost touching. "I don't know."

He stares into my eyes, studying me. "Cop-out. Come on. Be honest."

I've never talked about my feelings much. My foster family didn't want to know about how I felt about shit.

When my parents passed from my life, I did my very best to push down whatever feelings were trying to well up inside me.

"Nothing."

Stone takes my hand in his, continuing to watch me closely. "I want to hear it. You were talking, and then, boom…nothing. Something had to happen. Did someone upset you?"

I shake my head, pushing back the tears that are threatening to come. "It's silly, really."

"Opal," he says with a squeeze of my fingers, "it's not silly if it has you all out of sorts."

I swallow, hating myself for being so sappy in the company of others. "I was sitting here thinking that I wish I had been born into a family like this. Imagining how my life could be different. Even when my parents were around, it was never this good. It was just us. But to be surrounded by so many, loved by so many, it's pretty damn amazing. And if I'm being honest, I'm a little jealous too."

Stone's face softens as he gazes at me. "I'm sorry, Opal." His words hit me in the gut. No one's ever apologized for what I've gone through. Stone is the last person who should be apologizing to me, but his words provide a balm to a wound that I'm not sure will ever heal.

"It's not your fault," I tell him, trying to tune out the rambunctious conversation around us.

"It's not yours either."

"I know." I do my best to put a smile on my face, but it's lopsided before it falters.

"You're here now, though."

I want to say, yeah, I am, but for how long? Would I love to be here every week surrounded by such love and kindness? Fuck yeah.

"And they love you too. Probably more than they like me."

I laugh at those words. They give him so much shit, but he eats it up and feeds into it. "Don't be ridiculous. They love you."

"They put up with me."

"What's wrong?" his cousin Gigi asks, and the table stops talking, turning all their attention our way. "Do you guys need something? I'll grab it."

"No," I say to her, "everything is great."

"That's your great face?" Tamara asks with her eyebrows drawn down. "Looks pretty fucking serious to me."

"Back off," Stone barks, being a little too overprotective of my feelings.

It's my turn to squeeze his hand before turning back to his family around the table. "I'm just in awe of you guys. The love you have for one another. You're all so, so lucky."

"Not all of us," Rebel says to me with a small headshake. "I had a shit family until I married into this one."

"That ain't no fucking lie. I mean, my family was beyond fucked up and basically nonexistent until Gigi threw herself at me," Pike says, earning himself a smack to the shoulder.

"Babe, I never threw myself at you," she corrects him, giving him a wicked glare. "Don't lie."

"Besides the people born into this family, anyone here have a normal family?" Mammoth asks, glancing around at all of them.

One cousin raises his hand. "I did."

"Jett," Gigi groans. "You don't count."

"Why the fuck not?" Jett leans forward, placing his elbows on the table. "I wasn't born into this family."

"I've known you since we were both in diapers. Hell, our mothers were roommates. You're as close to being born into the family without being born into the family as there is."

"Dumb," he mutters, reaching for the beer in front of him.

"Where do we even begin with all the fucked-up shit we've been through?" Pike asks. "My mother was murdered because of my father."

Gigi touches Pike's arm. "Let's not forget how your father broke in to our apartment and tried to attack me."

My eyes widen. "What?" I ask, totally shocked.

"Yep." Gigi nods. "It was a crazy time."

"There're a lot of us who had no one—or if we did, we wished we didn't—before we met this family."

"Really?" I ask, still in disbelief.

"I do my best to forget everything that came before them," Rebel says to me. "It all seems to fade away because this family fills every void and hole you had before. You'll see."

"Maybe," I mumble, not able to imagine being one of them.

I can't barge right in and make myself at home. I'm here as a guest of Stone's grandparents because they're hoping Stone and I become a couple ending in marriage.

We barely know each other. Although my heart beats a little faster when he's nearby. I also feel comfortable in his presence, as if he's been part of my life forever. It's an odd thing to come to terms with because my heart and mind are at war with each other about what could be.

"She can come back, right?" Lily asks Stone. "We want her to come back."

"Yeah. Of course." Stone turns to me. "I want you to come back," he says genuinely as he tightens his grip on my hands.

"We'll see. We're not even…" My voice drifts off because I'm not sure what we are or where we're headed. We've never had a conversation about what's happening between us.

"Stone, are you seeing anyone else?" Lily asks him point-blank.

Stone shakes his head. "Only Opal."

"You ever date one person at a time?" she asks him.

"Nope."

Well, fuck. That's not good. He's never been able to date only one person at a time.

"Never been in a relationship until now."

My head snaps to him. "Never?" I ask, once again

shocked. Something that I'm getting used to feeling around him.

"No, babe. Never wanted to be in a relationship until now."

"So, we're a couple?" I ask him, confirming I'm not making more out of what's happening between us than is really there.

"Boom. Dating," Lily says with a clap. "You can thank me later by making me the maid of honor."

"Matron of honor," Gigi corrects her. "You're too damn old to be a maid, and you're married."

"Whatever," Lily says, practically bouncing in her chair.

"Wait," I say, turning my entire body toward Stone. "Don't let them bully you into dating me. You honestly don't have to. I'm okay with being alone. Been that way for a long time. I'm comfortable with it. Do you *want* to be in a relationship with me?"

He stares at me, his eyes roaming my face. "I do," he says with a smile. "I've never liked anyone else the way I like you."

"Aww," Nick, his cousin, says. "That's too damn sweet. It's almost gross."

Stone's gaze slices to Nick. "Shut it, man. I remember how pussy-whipped you were when you met Jo. You were a goddamn idiot."

Nick shrugs one shoulder. "Happens to the best of us. I'd do it all again too." He turns to his wife and pulls her close. "Would you?"

She moves her arms over his shoulders as she drapes her body against his. "Fuck yeah, baby. You're the best damn thing to happen to me."

I tune out the conversation, too busy thinking about the fact that Stone and I are apparently now a couple. But it's not because he asked me, but because his sister asked him. Was he backed into a corner and doesn't mean it?

How does a man who never wanted to be in a relationship now, all of a sudden, want to be in one? It's mind-boggling and truly unbelievable.

But sitting here, surrounded by these amazing people, I make a decision. I'm going to lie to myself and settle into the reality that I've found new people. I won't dwell on the likelihood that Stone will drop me like a hot potato when he gets bored with me.

"Hey," Stone says, nudging me. "Food's ready. You want me to grab a plate for you?"

"What?" I ask, still lost in thought.

"Want me to grab your food, or do you want to get your own?"

"Oh." My stomach gurgles, remembering the deliciousness of lunch on Friday. "I'll come in and get my own."

"Good. Come on. We'll go together," he says, pushing his chair back from the table.

I start to stand, and Stone moves the chair out for me before I can twist my body around the structure. "Thanks," I tell him, not used to such gentlemanly behavior.

"You sure you're okay?" he asks me, brushing my hair over my shoulder as I straighten.

"I'm good," I lie.

He tilts his head, looking at me with knitted brows. "I'm calling bullshit."

"Think whatever you want."

He gives a slow nod, and I think he's finally dropped the topic until we step into his grandparents' house and he hauls me down a hallway.

I don't even have time to notice if anyone has seen us as we passed by in a blur. "What are you doing?" I ask him.

He's not rough. There's a gentleness but also an urgency to his movements. "We're going to talk…alone."

"Oh boy," I mumble, following him through an open door. I glance around, realizing we're in a bedroom that looks like it hasn't been used in years. "About what?"

He closes the door but doesn't lock it and doesn't block my way out. "What happened out there?"

I stare at him, blinking a few times to stall. "Nothing happened."

"You were sad, happy, and then sad again."

I shrug with a sigh. "It's my own bullshit."

He marches up to me and places a hand on each shoulder. "It's our bullshit now."

I gawk at him, a little stunned. "Since when?"

"Since I made you my girl."

"Since you made me your girl?" I repeat, but I turn the last word up into a question.

He nods as he brushes his thumbs back and forth against my shoulders. "Yep. So, whatever's bothering you now bothers me."

"Stone."

"I'm serious, Opal."

"I don't want to be in a relationship with you because your sister put you on the spot. That's not how it should be."

He hangs his head for a moment. "I'm an asshole."

I lift my arms until my hands are on his abdomen. A very nice, tight, and muscular abdomen. "No, you're not."

He glances up, giving me his entire attention. "I should've made shit clearer before we got here. I didn't say that because my sister wanted me to. I said that because I wanted to. I was too scared to say something before, thinking you'd tell me to kick rocks."

"Kick rocks? What's that even mean?"

Stone smiles. "It's like get lost."

I'm horrified he'd think that. "Why in the world would I tell you to kick rocks?"

"I know Jeff left a bad taste in your mouth, and I thought maybe you wanted more time to…"

I know where he's going with this, and a few weeks ago, I would've agreed. But I've had enough time, and there's no perfect time anyway. "I don't want more time. I've spent most of my life alone, and I'm over Jeff. If I'm honest, I was over him before we ended. I know what I want. Who I want. And that's you."

"I want you too, Opal. I've never done this before, so

just know I will fuck up, but I'll do my best to be the best for you. You deserve more than a shithead like me."

I lean into him, smashing myself against him as his arms crumple before sliding around my shoulders. "You don't have to be the very best." I hug him tightly, pressing my cheek into his pecs. "I just want you."

He sets his chin on top of my head. "I was scared, and that's not easy for me to admit. I haven't stopped thinking about you. I can't get you out of my damn mind sometimes. It's scary as hell for me."

"It's not easy for me either." Opening up my life to someone surrounded by so much love is frightening.

What if I not only fall in love with him, but his entire family too, and then we end? Shit. It would destroy me.

"What just ran through your mind?"

"Nothing."

"Babe, you went from a pile of goo to stiff as a board in a split second."

I sag into him, willing myself to relax. "It's stupid."

"I'm the king of stupid. Give me a try."

"I don't want to make you feel bad."

"I'm a rock."

I turn my head, pressing the front of my face into his soft T-shirt. "It's a lot. It's heavy."

"Have you seen my muscles?" he teases. "I can take it."

I peer up, soaking in the hard edges of his jaw. "I like your family as much as I like you."

I'm being partially truthful, but not entirely. The last

thing I'd want is for him to stay with me out of pity. And if I voice the thought I had in that second, it'll happen.

I know it will, and that's the last thing I want.

"I love that," he breathes into my hair. "Because I'm around them a lot. A stupid amount of time. And if you hated them, that would make shit hard and uncomfortable for everyone involved."

"Yeah?"

"Yeah." He smiles down at me, making my belly do a few backflips. "And now you're going to be around them a lot too. Probably so much you'll get sick of them after a while."

"I find that hard to believe."

"You'll see. They'll make you a little bit off your rocker."

"Who said I was on it already?" I ask him, wrapping my arms around his thick middle until my fingers barely slide together.

The man is big, probably bigger than anyone else I've ever been with. He's the first person who's made me feel small in his arms, and that offers me a sliver of safety I've never felt before.

He laughs again, making my entire body shake. "You want kids someday?" he asks out of freaking nowhere.

"What?" I ask, my entire body stiffening again, but not out of fear.

"You want kids someday?" He pulls back, staring down at me.

I blink a few times, trying to let his words penetrate my

brain. I've wanted a family for as long as I can remember. Growing up alone made me long for a ton of kids running around me. I never wanted anyone else to experience what I had. "Someday, yeah."

"How many?"

"Two," I whisper, but really it's more than double that.

"You good with at least four?"

I'm almost stunned speechless. "You want four kids?" I wheeze out, hoping I don't hyperventilate.

"At least. Maybe more. It'll depend on how quick we get started because I don't want to be using a walker when the last one graduates from high school."

I laugh at that mental image. "You don't want the other kids to think you're the grandpa?"

"God, no. That would be awful. If we start soon, then maybe something like five or six. You good with that?"

"I can't believe we're talking about this." I want to pull away from him and pace around the room to burn off the mini freak-out I'm experiencing.

He tightens his hands around my waist. "I'm not playing around, Opal. I want you to know I'm serious about us. Dead-fucking-serious. I'm not talking short-term. I want to go the distance."

"How does a man never date and then talk about having an entire baseball team of kids with someone?"

"When you know, you know," he says casually. "I knew the other ones weren't for me, but the moment I laid eyes on you, I knew you were the one. I gave you some time to work out whatever you needed to work out, but now we're together and I'm pressing on that gas, making sure I don't let you slip through my fingers because I'm not the smoothest when it comes to this stuff."

"You're pretty smooth, big guy." Smooth enough that he already got me naked, and it didn't take a declaration of love to make that happen either.

I'd never been the type to sleep with someone without at least some sort of commitment, but Stone had his way with me way too easily. I knew then I was a goner for him. I tilt my neck back, looking up at him. "At least you are with me."

He brushes his lips against mine so softly that I barely feel them. "Make me earn it, Opal. Don't go easy on me. I want only the best for you, and when I'm being a shithead, I want you to call me out on it. Got me?"

"I'll try."

"Stay with me tonight."

"Okay," I say way too easily and quickly.

He smirks. "I'm going to give you so many orgasms, you're going to pass out."

"Don't threaten me with a good time."

"You're going to scream my name tonight, baby."

"Fuck," I moan, thinking about the things he did to my body last time.

"I plan on it," he promises as he moves his hands to my ass. "Now, let's fill that belly because you're going to burn a lot of calories tonight."

"Thanks," I whisper.
"For what?"
"For saving me."

15

STONE

"You really went for it, didn't you?" Pike asks me as soon as I sit down at my station. "Didn't mess around at all."

"You said lock it down, and I locked it down."

Pike leans back, staring at me with a smug smile. "You listened. You never listen to anything I say."

I rub my temples, trying to relieve the headache he's giving me. "I always listen to you."

Pike laughs. "Do you believe your own bullshit?"

I cross my arms, staring at him. "If you keep giving me shit, I won't listen ever again."

Pike raises his hands. "I'm not giving you any shit."

"Any *more* shit," I correct him.

"How's my baby brother?" Lily asks as she walks into the back of the shop carrying an extra-large coffee, which is no doubt filled with sugar.

"He's a bit grumpy," Pike tells her, earning himself another glare. "See?" He waves a hand in my direction.

Lily laughs. "Why the hell are you grumpy? You looked happy when you left after dinner yesterday."

"I'm not grumpy. Jesus," I groan.

"Oh yeah. You sound happy as a clam," Lily says as she plops into a chair across from me. "What's Opal up to today?

"She's meeting with Tamara this morning."

"Oh yeah. I forgot about that." Lily smiles. "Everything's falling into place."

"What's falling into place?"

"Your future." She rocks her head back and forth, looking so damn happy. "Our future."

I laugh and shake my head. My sister is such a weirdo. Always has been and probably always will be. But that's what I love about her. She marches to her own drum and doesn't give a flying fuck what anyone else thinks. "What the hell does it have to do with your future?"

"You're growing up, settling down."

The phone rings at the front desk, and Lily sets down her coffee before stalking away without me being able to argue with her.

I'm fully grown, no matter what she thinks. Settling down? Why do we use that term? It sounds like someone's giving up instead of moving forward with their life.

"I like her," Rebel says as she strolls through the back room, tidying up whatever we didn't do before we closed up the shop on Saturday night. "I think you're good for each other."

"I think she's better for me than I am for her."

Rebel stops moving and spins around to face me. "Stone, you don't understand what life is like for her. You never could, no matter how hard you try. But don't sell yourself short. You may be part meathead and an asshole, but to Opal, none of that matters when you're showing her the love she deserves."

I fidget with my tools, hating talking about this shit with my cousins. They've always gone on and on about their feelings, but it's never been my thing. I'm not as open as them, and I'm not sure I ever will be.

"Stone, your customer canceled today. They're sick," Lily says as she walks back to where I'm sitting. "You're free most of the day."

"Fuck," I groan. "He had a six-hour appointment. He was my entire day."

Lily shrugs like it's no big deal. "Why don't you take the day off and take your girl for lunch or something?"

I want to tell her to butt out and mind her own business, but her idea isn't bad. There's no point in my sitting here, waiting for some random person who will walk into the shop and need a cheap little tattoo. It rarely happens and isn't worth the aggravation. On top of that, everyone here will want to talk about Opal and our future together.

"I think I will," I tell her, earning myself the biggest smile from my sister. "Anything's better than sitting here and listening to you all whine today."

"I'm not whining," Lily says as she swipes her coffee from the workstation table. "Life's too good right now."

"Hush up," Gigi says to Lily. "Don't jinx shit."

"I don't believe in that."

Gigi stands over my sister, one hand on her hip, shaking her head. "You'll see. You opened someone up for a world of hurt with your nonsense, Lily."

Lily gulps down her coffee, rolling her eyes.

"I'm out," I tell them, happy I don't have to listen to their shit for an entire day.

"Have fun," Lily says to me as I stand from my chair.

"Go get her, tiger," Pike teases me.

I give them all the finger before I stalk into the customer waiting room and out the front door. I glance up, letting the bright sunshine warm my face.

And then it happens.

I realize my life is changing. I'm making plans for the future, when I used to fly by the seat of my pants. I thrived on the uncertainty and the freedom I had to do whatever, whenever.

Am I okay with the change? I think so.

Am I petrified of the change? Abso-fucking-lutely.

I reach for my phone and message the woman who has my mind and body in a complete jumble.

Me: When will you be done?

I head to my truck, climbing inside the cab, and put the air conditioning on full blast. I sit there for a minute, waiting for the cold air to start flowing before putting the truck in drive.

Opal: About an hour. Why? Aren't you working?

Me: Appointment canceled. I'll pick you up at your place in two hours.

It's the perfect day. The sun is shining, the sky is a brilliant blue, and there isn't a cloud overhead. There's only one place I want to take her.

Opal: Where are we going?

Me: Wear your suit and bring your sunscreen. We're going to the beach.

Opal: Oh, wow. Okay. I'll be waiting!

I smile to myself. The day is a win-win for me. Not only am I going to give Opal an experience she's never had before, but she's going to do it in a hot little bikini.

I spend the next hour getting all the shit we'll need to spend the day in the sun. I grab the best subs from the local grocery store, drinks, and snacks so that we can spend an entire day on the sand. I throw a giant umbrella into the back of my truck for when the sun becomes too much and a blanket. I even grab a bottle of wine to sip while we watch the sunset over the Gulf.

As soon as everything's loaded, I stop moving, looking over all the supplies in the truck bed. "Who am I?" I ask myself, but no one else answers. "I'm a fucking pansy."

"No, handsome, you're a man in love," my neighbor says from beside her car. "It's nice to know love isn't dead in this day and age."

I smile at her, taking in the lines on her face and whiteness of her hair. "No, ma'am, love isn't dead, but it's terrifying as hell."

"Nothing worth a damn is easy. You need to lean into the uncomfortable and embrace the ride."

She sounds like a mix of my grandparents and parents. Full of wisdom and flowery advice. But I don't argue with her, just like I don't argue with them. They've lived longer, experienced more, and have a knowledge base I can only dream of having myself one day.

"You have a good day, ma'am."

She smiles at me. "Enjoy yourself."

"I plan too," I say with a wink.

She waves her hand at me, chuckling to herself as she walks away, wobbling with each step.

I don't waste another minute. The last thing I want to do is be late in picking up Opal. Punctuality has never been my strong suit, but with her, I want to be my best.

When I pull up at Opal's, she's standing outside looking every bit delicious. She's wearing a flowy dress with her hair tied back but spilling over her shoulder. Her legs are bare, and I can't stop myself from daydreaming about them being wrapped around my waist.

She walks toward my truck, and I hop out, running around the front to get the door for her. My father taught me how to be a gentleman, but I've never bothered until now. Opal changed that in me. The switch flipped, and now I'm not sure there's any going back.

"You look beautiful," I tell her as she walks in front of me, leaving her scent in her wake. My knees go weak because I want to taste her, but now isn't the time or the place.

"Thank you," she says, glancing over her shoulder at me as her eyes drop to my chest. "You're looking pretty beautiful yourself."

I look down, realizing, in my haste, I forgot to put on a shirt. Doesn't matter. Where we're going, clothing isn't required. "You like what you see, baby?"

"No better sight."

"I thought you liked my pretty face," I tease.

"I love the entire package," she says with a wink.

My cock twitches in appreciation, a little overeager for the day to come. But I learned a long time ago, sand and sex do not mix. It's a recipe for disaster and pain. One I'm not about to replicate.

She stops at the door of the truck, waiting for me to open it for her. "Where are we headed?"

I peer down at her, casting a shadow over her small frame. "A little beach not far from here. It's private, and usually there aren't many people there."

"Sounds perfect." She climbs up with a little help from me before making herself comfortable and placing her bag of things next to her feet.

"It will be," I promise her before closing the door. I'm halfway around the front of the truck when I start talking to myself again. "Don't be an idiot. Do not blow this today."

I'd like to pretend I've been smooth my entire life, but that would be a complete lie. I fuck up more shit than should be humanly possible. Somehow, I've lived through it all and never really cared, but with Opal, I want to make things right. She's had enough bad in her life, and I never want to add to it.

"Ready?" I ask her as soon as I'm back in the front with her next to me.

"I've never been more ready for anything." She lifts her arm, reaching over to where my hand's resting on the console. "Thank you for this."

"For what, babe? A beach day?"

She nods. "For wanting to spend it with me and take me somewhere I've never been."

"I want to show you all the things in life you've never experienced."

"You've already done that more than you can ever imagine."

I haven't done shit. Nothing at all. The bare minimum, and yet, she's giving me props for it. That's some messed-up shit.

I turn my body, leaning my back against the driver's door. "Honest question, and please don't take this the wrong way, but have all your boyfriends been absolute shit?"

She plays with the hem of her dress, staring down at her legs. "I didn't have many, but I guess the simple answer is yes."

"That's sad," I tell her, but then I remember I fall into that category for a lot of women I've been with.

I did as little as I could get away with, wanting nothing more than to get in their pants and move on. I have some atonement to do, and I'll spend all that energy on Opal, doing my best to give her everything she deserves.

Is it because she's missed out on so much? Maybe. She is like finding that stray kitten, wanting to give it love, saving it from a life of sadness and despair. But that isn't all of it. I've never given a shit about what other people are going through, but Opal's different in my eyes.

"I think it's more the norm. I don't think my lived experience with men is very different from other women. *You're* just different, Stone."

"I'm really not, or at least, I wasn't."

"What happened before me doesn't count. We all change and grow up, figuring out what we want and who we are. You're finding yourself, and I'm lucky enough to be with you while you are."

"Does it scare you?"

She looks at me funny. "Does what scare me?"

"That you're with me while I'm figuring out who I am."

She shakes her head and smiles in a way that eases any anxiety I'm feeling. "Not at all. We're both figuring shit out together."

"You make me want to be the best version of me," I admit. "But you need to know I'm going to mess up from time to time."

"So will I. I don't know how to be with someone who goes above and beyond and is nice."

Those words make my heart hurt. I see pain behind her

blue eyes, and the smile she has plastered on her face is more about her resiliency than the experience.

I reach over, wrapping my hand around the back of her neck, and pull her toward me. She moves without hesitation, keeping her gaze locked on mine as her face comes closer.

"I want this forever," I tell her, never having had something so easy with another person. "I want you forever."

"I want it too," she breathes, sending a shock wave of excitement and nervous energy throughout my body. "I want this. I want you."

When my lips find hers, the sparks grow, causing goose bumps to scatter across my skin. I'm bombarded by the warmth of her skin, the sweetness of her scent, and the nearness of her.

What should've been a gentle, slow kiss turns into something almost feral. It's a mess of lips, tongues, and moans. I could get lost in the moment, allowing my need for her to take over.

But I pull away, gasping for air. "We can't."

Her eyes flutter open, her lips still puckered. "What?"

"We're going to the beach, babe. If we kiss any more, we're not going to make it out of your parking lot."

"Can we kiss at the beach?" she asks me, her lips all bee-stung from our moment.

"We sure as hell can."

"Then let's get going. We have an ocean to get to and some making out to happen."

"I like your style, Opal," I tell her, twisting my body

INFERNO

back into place and putting the truck in drive. "It'll be a day you'll never forget."

"Every day with you is like that, Stone." She places her hand back on my arm as I drive. "I don't know how I got so lucky."

The opposite is true. She's the chillest woman I've ever met, and for that, I'll forever be thankful. Maybe I needed someone calm to bring me down a notch or two. I no longer want to party, because nothing is better than making Opal smile and watching her light up when she experiences true joy.

I do that for her, and I'll do my best to keep that look on her face.

16

OPAL

"It's so beautiful," I whisper as I lean against Stone, tucked between his legs with my toes buried in the sand.

I haven't been able to take my eyes off the horizon as the sun slowly sets, growing larger and the colors becoming more brilliant.

"It looks like a postcard," I add, completely in awe.

Stone's arms tighten around me as he rests his chin on my shoulder and his head next to mine. "This is my favorite place."

"I can see why."

The few people on the beach around us have become still, captivated by the same view. Every second, the sky changes, shifting between colors like a kaleidoscope.

This moment is too good, too peaceful. Whenever my life appears to be falling into place, I wait for the other shoe to drop and squash everything. It always happens.

Every single time I feel like things are swinging my way, boom…reality smacks me in the face. I push the thought out of my mind, trying to keep the bad away from all this good.

This time will be different.

"Thank you for today."

His lips find my neck, sending a cascade of goose bumps and shivers down my body. "I want to show you all the beautiful things you've been missing."

Been missing? I've missed so many things my entire adult life. So many things, I'm not even sure where to start. As they say, you don't know what you don't know, and I don't know a hell of a lot.

It's as if I've lived two separate lives—before my parents died and after. When they were there, they made sure I knew exactly how much they loved me, showering me with love. But afterward, I only remember darkness. The feelings of loneliness were so overwhelming at times, I couldn't imagine them ever going away.

I pull myself forward and shift my body until I'm facing Stone. I tuck my legs under myself and move as close as I can without smashing my front against him. "Why are you being so good to me?"

He raises his hand and moves a few wild hairs away from my eyes. "I don't get the question." He tilts his head, the sunset reflecting in his eyes. "What do you mean?"

I find the bare skin of his shoulders with my hands, feeling the heat from today's sun against my palms. "You don't have to be perfect all the time."

His eyebrows draw inward. "No one's perfect all the time, Opal, and I'm not an exception."

"You're perfect to me," I whisper, letting my fingers inch farther up his shoulder to his neck.

"That'll wear off." He smiles down at me, making me feel like I'm the only woman in the world.

"I can't imagine it ever will."

I haven't had as much attention and caring from anyone since my parents. And if I am being totally honest with myself, it scares the ever-living daylights out of me.

"Why me?"

"Why not you?"

I shake my head, unable to answer the question.

"Why me?" he asks me.

"Why not you?" I tease.

His arms find their way around me again. "Do you believe in fate or love at first sight?"

"I never did until…"

"Until us?" He raises a single eyebrow, waiting for my confirmation.

I swallow, remembering all the feels he's kicked up in me since the day he pushed Jeff out of the shop. I was immediately drawn to Stone, wanting nothing more than for him to be in my life. I fought every feeling I had, thinking it was too early or that I wasn't worthy.

"There was something about you that drew me in."

"My good looks have a way of doing that to people."

I laugh at his egotistical nonsense. The man is the most confident person I know, and I love that about him.

"But do you think there are people who are meant for each other?" he asks again.

"Maybe."

"Do you think *we* were meant for each other?" I ask.

"I think if I could have created someone for me, I would've created you."

17

STONE

"Hey," I say, walking into ALFA and seeing my aunt Angel's smiling face.

"Hey, sunshine. What brings you by?" She stands and rounds her desk to come toward me.

"Uncle James called and asked me to drop by." He was cagey on the phone, wanting to see me in person, which is completely unlike him.

Other than today, I've come to ALFA maybe five times in my entire life. Always with my father when he wanted to drop in and see what his brothers were up to. I think he secretly wanted to get into some shit with them because he is such an adrenaline junkie. I'm surprised he didn't go into the same line of work, but I'm pretty sure my mom made certain that didn't happen.

"Oh," she says as she embraces me, followed by a light kiss on each cheek. "That's strange."

"Yeah," I say with a hint of laughter because it's not

only strange, it's suspicious as hell. "They treating you right around here, Auntie? If not, we could use your skills over at Inked to keep everything in order."

She pats my arm as she laughs. "Honey, the men around here would crumble if I left. Everything would seize up and stop working. Don't even get me started on their inability to find anything, even if it's marked clear as day."

I laugh too, but I'm guilty of the exact same thing. It has to be tied to male hormones or how our brains are structured. We're definitely missing something that most women seem to have in spades. "The offer is always open."

"Stone?" My uncle's voice booms down the long hallway.

My smile dies. "He doesn't sound happy."

Aunt Angel swats her hand toward the hall. "The man's been sporting a sour puss all day. But you know James. He's all bark and no bite."

"Is he?" I don't want to tell her I've heard way too many rumors about him and Uncle Thomas to believe they're all made-up. They have a dark past that's been swept under the rug and forgotten about by everyone in their lives. "You sure about that?"

Angel laughs again. "Yes, honey. He's like a giant golden retriever."

I want to argue and pick another breed. One that lures you in with its good looks before snapping off your fingers with its powerful jaw.

"Now, go," Angel says, shooing me in the direction of the offices. "Don't leave without saying goodbye."

I give her a quick nod, not waiting around another minute before stalking down the hallway to Uncle James's office. When I push open the door, Uncle Thomas is sitting across from him, and they're each staring at papers inside manila folders.

"Hey, kid. Take a seat," James says, pointing to the seat next to Uncle Thomas.

"Hi," I say, sounding like a freaking idiot. "What's up, guys?" I don't wait to be told again because the look on Uncle James's face is pure business. "Long time no see." I can't help myself with the stupid words. I'm used to sitting with them to watch a football game, but this is something else entirely.

"I got a call last night," Uncle James says, placing the folder on his desk and giving me his full attention.

I glance to my side, but Thomas isn't looking at me. He's too busy flipping papers.

Uncle James clears his throat, wanting my attention, and I give it to him. "A buddy of mine in the police department called because your name came up more than a few times."

I swallow as dread comes over me. "Am I in trouble?"

Uncle James leans back in his chair and rubs his hands together. "No, son. A few of their residents," he says, as if he isn't talking about inmates at the county jail, "heard rumblings from another resident that there was a threat on your life."

I jerk my head back, surprised by this news. I wouldn't say I'm shocked. I think there're a lot of men out there with a hard-on for me. Either I stole their girl, or I beat their ass and they can't think about anything else except payback. "Me? Who?"

He reaches for the folder again. "Jeff—" he pauses, staring at the paperwork "—Shepard. You know him?"

My blood runs cold. "That's Opal's ex. Fuck him."

Those words draw Uncle Thomas's attention. "Interesting."

"What's interesting?" I ask him.

He runs a hand across his dark beard, something he's been growing out for far too long, based on the unkempt looks of it. "He has a major hard-on for you. You steal Opal away from him?"

I shake my head. "No. He was a client at the shop. He treated her like shit, so I told him to leave and explained that his business wasn't needed or wanted in our establishment. Afterward, I gave Opal a place to stay for a night, and then we barely talked for a month."

Thomas digs his fingers into the hair of his beard, scratching at the little bit of skin he can reach. "From the sounds of it, he puts the blame squarely on your shoulders."

"He brought that shit on himself—and the jail time too."

Uncle Thomas gives me a slow nod, but not the type that's reassuring in any way. "He has a court date tomorrow. He could get out, and then we have a high probability that shit might go down."

"I'd like to see that little pissant try. I could beat his ass with one hand tied behind my back and blindfolded."

"Do you think he'll act on the threats, or do you think he's just talking big since he's surrounded by other criminals?" Uncle James asks Uncle Thomas. "I want to know if we should put men on Stone—and Opal too."

"No men on me," I tell him, refusing to have anyone put their life on the line for mine. I can take care of myself. My dad has been teaching me self-defense and how to fight since the day I could hurl my fist through the air and land it without toppling over. "I can take care of myself."

Uncle James winces. "Listen, kid, I know you can. But when there's a nutjob coming after you with nothing but hate, it's harder to defend yourself. One set of eyes is never enough. Let me put at least two guys on you."

Fuck. If Jeff doesn't kill me, he better be prepared to die himself. There's no way I'm letting him get away with attacking me or Opal and live to breathe another day.

"Put everyone on Opal," I tell him, clenching my hands into tight fists. "She needs the protection, not me."

James folds his hands together, tapping his index fingers to each other. "If he gets released, take her to your place at night, and we'll put some guys on the outside. It's the best of both worlds."

"Do you think he'll actually get released?" I ask in disbelief.

James nods. "The jails are overcrowded, and it's a first

offense. He'll probably walk with time served, community service, and probation."

"Unbelievable," I mutter. "We need to tell Tamara."

"Fuck, that's right," Thomas says as he tosses the manila folder onto James's desk. "Opal's working with her, and that puts Tamara in danger too."

"It puts everyone she's around in danger," James adds. "How do we want to deal with this? Should we tell everyone?"

Thomas shakes his head. "No. I don't want to cause panic. The guy's probably talking big to make himself appear stronger than he is, or am I reading him wrong?"

"He put a tracker on her car. Mammoth found it. That's why his ass is in jail," I inform them.

Thomas stands from his chair and walks around the room. "The threat was against Stone and not Opal."

"I can take care of myself," I repeat, trying to drive the point home.

Uncle Thomas stops behind me and places his hand on my shoulder. "We know you're tough, Stone. Anyone with eyes can see you can easily take down most men out there in the world. But all the muscles in the world can't stop a bullet from piercing flesh. You got me?"

"I got you," I grumble, hating that he's right.

Thomas releases his hold on my shoulders before pacing back and forth. "Maybe you and she should go away for a few days until we assess the threat and see if he was talking out of his ass or if he really plans on following through."

"No. We're not going to run," I tell them, refusing to be a coward. "I've never been the type to run from trouble."

"Were we this stupid at his age?" James asks Thomas.

"Dumber," he replies with a small chuckle. "It's amazing we're still standing here."

"Self-preservation wasn't always our strong suit," James says like they're talking about something mundane and not death.

"Did either of you ever have anything like this happen to you?"

Their eyes turn to me, and the air in the room changes.

"Something like this," James says.

I glance between them, wondering what I don't know and they've never bothered to share.

"Yeah," Thomas adds. "We led different lives back then, but we were also trained in how to protect ourselves."

"My dad trained me," I remind them, crossing my arms over my chest.

"You may be able to protect yourself, but who's going to protect Opal while you're busy?" Uncle Thomas asks, making a good point even if I hate it.

"Don't let your ego be the death of one of you," Uncle James adds.

His statement is like a punch to the gut. Am I letting my ego get in the way? I suppose I am. Could my ego get one of us killed? It's entirely possible. I've never needed anyone to protect me since I was little, but I've never had anyone coming after me either. Jeff has had nothing but time in jail to sit and think of all the ways he could harm me. A few ideas are probably things I couldn't even come up with in my wildest dreams.

I run my fingers back and forth through my hair on a long exhale. "Fine. I'll tell Opal about everything tonight, and you let us know if he gets released. We'll figure it out then, okay?"

"You got it, kid." Thomas finally looks pleased, which, for him, means he isn't brooding for once. "We'll start making moves on our end, lining shit up just in case, and you inform Opal and make some plans of your own. He gets released, we'll meet up and hammer out the final details until we know he's no longer a threat. Got it?"

"Ridiculous," I mutter, earning myself a glare from Uncle James. "Yeah. I'll tell Opal and make some decisions."

"Good." Uncle James smiles.

"Should we keep this between us, at least for now?" I ask, glancing back and forth between them.

"We'll talk that over. Anyone around you could be at risk, so we must do what's right if you're not willing to leave town."

"I'll tell everyone at the shop."

James nods. "I'll tell your parents and the others, but I don't think we should worry your grandparents yet."

"Are people going to keep that secret?" I ask with a raised eyebrow. "You know how they are."

"This is one secret they'll keep. When someone's in

danger, it's amazing how quickly their lips snap shut and stay that way."

"If you say so, but since everything has been calm with no threats in forever, you don't really know that that's true."

James smiles. "There've been threats, and the fact that you don't know about them means everyone kept their damn mouths closed."

I'm shocked back into my chair. "Really? Who?"

James shakes his head as he shifts around the papers on his desk. "It's not important."

"Whatever," I mumble. "Someday I want the full story on the family."

"It could fill books, Stone. Way more books than you could ever imagine," Thomas states. "Now, we have other shit to do today."

That's my cue to leave. "Thanks for filling me in on everything. I'll handle my shit on my end." I stand, ready to figure out how I'm going to protect both of us and put an end to Jeff.

"Don't do anything stupid," Uncle Thomas says like he's reading my damn mind.

"Never," I lie. "I always use my head."

Uncle Thomas's lips flatten. "No, you don't. It's not genetically possible."

"Watch your back," James warns.

"Always," I promise them.

Angel's on her feet before I make it to the waiting

room. "Everything okay?" she asks me with a nervous smile.

"Yeah. I think so. They'll fill you in later, Auntie."

She pulls me into a hug, longer than the one she gave me when I arrived. "You take care of yourself, kiddo. Don't be a stranger."

I pull back, looking at her beautiful face framed by her signature red hair. "I see you every weekend."

She laughs. "I know, but it's good to see your face in this office. It's a nice change of pace from the usual guys."

"I'll drop in more often," I promise her, giving her a kiss on the cheek. "Anything to brighten your day."

"You're the best, Stone."

"I know," I tell her, getting a smack on the arm and a round of laughter.

"Totally Gallo," she mumbles.

"That ain't no lie," I say, giving her a wave over my shoulder as I stalk toward the entrance and push into the damp, hot air, ready for whatever's about to come.

18

OPAL

"What if he succeeds?" I ask Stone as he pulls my tank top over my head, trying to alleviate my stress by getting me naked.

It's working too.

Every spot his hand touches pushes the fear further from my mind. His lips drive away all the worrisome thoughts that have been cycling through my brain since he filled me in on the threats to his life.

"He won't," he murmurs against my neck as he slides his palms up my sides.

I shiver as his fingertips brush against my spine. "How do you know?"

"Shh," Stone says, nudging my hair back with his face to get better access to my neck. "Forget about him."

I'm not really thinking about Jeff, but about us and how we're going to get through this with my ex coming after us. I wonder if he'll ever forget I exist and move on with his life. I thought he had the first night when I went to get my things, but I was completely wrong.

Stone's fingers find the back of my strapless bra, making quick and easy work of the clasps. The restrictive material falls to the floor, and I let out a little moan from the relief. "I like you better without that," he says and cups my breasts. "You should never cage them. Not for me."

"They're kind of required for society," I tell him, grasping his biceps to steady myself and stay standing.

"Society is bullshit. They're too beautiful. Too soft," he whispers as his lips trail down the front of my throat, heading toward my breasts.

I lean back, making it easier for him to put his mouth anywhere and everywhere he wants. I give myself to him, knowing he's going to make every awful thing that's plaguing my thoughts vanish.

Stone takes a step forward, bringing me with him. He bends, laying me over the edge of the couch. Before I can say anything, he's kneeling on the floor, working on the button of my jeans.

"I need you naked," he says as he pops the button and then yanks at the zipper.

I run my fingertips over the swells of my breasts. "But you forgot about these," I tease him.

His eyes shift, meeting mine, and darken. "I haven't forgotten, babe. I don't want any barrier between us."

I play with the hair on the top of his head as he pulls down my jeans, struggling a little around my ankles.

"I hate skinny jeans," he grumbles, finally yanking the second leg off.

I hold in my laughter because I've had the same thought a million times, but they make my ass look fabulous. They're a double-edged sword.

He tosses my jeans behind him. Any words I was going to say die when his soft, warm lips find the edge of my silk panties, pressing into my flesh. "I've missed this."

"Me too," I breathe, leaning back, finding it harder to keep myself steady.

He makes my entire body weak, and I'm not sure I'll ever get enough of him.

Stone's quick to stand, pressing against my shoulder to mold my back to the rounded armrest of the couch. "Don't move," he tells me as I stare up at the ceiling with my vagina almost up in the air.

He spreads my legs wide, leaving me a little vulnerable and exposed. He brings his palm down on my breast, cupping my flesh tenderly.

"Fuck," he moans, undoing his pants with one hand and kicking them off without a problem. "You're so goddamn beautiful." I start to close my legs, but he pushes his body between them, stopping me. "No, baby. No hiding what's mine."

His words rachet up my need, making me want to rub my legs together to alleviate the sensation. But Stone presses his length against me, sending an electric jolt from my clit all across my body.

I gasp, wanting more…needing more.

Stone leans over, his hand still on my breast, cock pressed against me, and places his lips on mine. I open my mouth to him and widen my legs, wanting everything he has to give me.

"Greedy," he murmurs against my mouth.

I kiss him deeper, wrapping my legs around his body to hold him to me. I move my hips, rubbing my middle against him, wanting the friction...needing the contact.

"You're mine, Opal. Only mine," he growls as he pushes his cock inside me and starts to move.

I'm left speechless and panting, feeling his words inside my soul.

"Only yours," I whisper back to him, wrapping my arms around his shoulders to hold my body as tightly as I can around his.

We move together in perfect sync, driving each other close to the edge. My hands roam across his back, memorizing every inch of him, wishing I could watch him as he makes love to me.

Is this love? I think so. I've never felt anything like this before.

I allow myself to get lost in the feeling of him, pushing away any thoughts of love or worries about the future.

Now is all that matters.

The way his cock fills me.

The way his body fits with mine.

The way his gaze has the power to steal my breath.

It's as if we were meant to be here...together.

INFERNO

Everything that came before Stone doesn't exist.
It's only us.
Only him.
I close my eyes, letting my entire world be filled with him, and wish we could be like this forever.

19

STONE

"This is a little over the top." Opal gazes down at her makeshift workstation, tapping her foot. "How am I supposed to work here?" She waves her hand around the busy shop. "It's loud."

"It's public and safe," I tell her.

She peers up at me, eyes narrowed. "I'd be perfectly safe at Nuts & Bolts with Mammoth, Tamara, and Nick."

"I can't do my job from there, but you can do yours from here."

The pink in her cheeks deepens. "Ridiculous," she mutters.

"Hey, Opal. It's good to see you," Trace says, giving me a chin lift as he walks by.

"Hey, Trace," she says, but her voice is flat. She hasn't taken her eyes off me. "What if I refuse?"

"I'm not letting you out of my sight, babe. Where you go, I go. He's on the streets and could be anywhere."

"I doubt he'll try something this fast."

I tilt my head as I cross my arms over my chest. "Are you willing to risk it? You think he has some timeline in his head he's following?" I pause, holding up a single finger. "Or is there some manual on stalker etiquette?"

She inhales deeply, holding in her breath for a few seconds before exhaling. "You're so stubborn."

Gigi slaps her leg and laughs. "This is better than a reality TV show."

"Shut up," I tell my cousin. "I could use a little help instead of heckling."

Gigi gives me an eye roll. "He's right," she grumbles. "It's better to be safe than sorry. You're both safer surrounded by all of us than on your own."

"I wasn't going to be on my own. I was going to be at Nuts & Bolts."

"Not enough people and Mammoth gets busy. I know Tamara can kick some serious ass, but even she has her limits. And would you really want to put them in danger for no reason?" Gigi asks Opal.

Opal hangs her head, kicking the toe of her shoe against the tile. "I didn't think of it that way, but now you're all at risk."

"There's no better place for you to be," Gigi says, looking around the room. "You have a lot of people who've been through a lot of shit and aren't afraid to get a little dirty."

"I guess." Opal straightens her back, letting out another loud exhale.

"If you want," Gigi says, looking toward the back of the shop, "you can set up in the office to have a little more privacy."

"No," I snap. "Here's fine."

"I'd love to work in the office," Opal says, overriding my decision because of Gigi's idea.

"Fuck," I growl. "The office will work, but keep the door open."

Opal's face changes. "Thank you," she whispers before popping up on her toes to kiss my cheek.

I lean over, giving her full access to my face. "Don't make me regret it."

"You're a pain in the ass," she murmurs against my skin.

"I'm just trying to keep us alive."

"I'm not looking to die anytime soon." Her hand finds my bicep, and she digs her fingers into my muscle. "We have things to do together."

I raise an eyebrow as I gaze down at her. "Dirty things?"

"Is there anything else?" Opal says with a laugh. "All the things."

"Anal?" I ask, but I know the answer already.

"Never," she replies.

"People can hear you," Gigi chimes in before making a gagging sound. "So gross."

Opal's face lights up. "I love your family."

"We love you too," Gigi tells her.

"I second that," Rebel says, popping her head into the back area.

"They're so nosy, though," I tell Opal.

"And bossy...like you." Opal smiles at me as she moves toward her laptop, snatching it up and heading to the office without a second glance.

"Lay off a bit. Give her a little space," Gigi tells me.

"Don't do that," Pike says. "Shit's too dangerous right now. We've been there, done that."

"Come on," Gigi grumbles. "You're all overreacting."

"Darlin'," Pike drawls, leaning back in his chair, looking relaxed and calm, "We've been in their shoes. There's no such thing as overreacting. They let their guard down, and they could end up dead."

"You're overdramatic," Gigi says to him, shaking her head to herself.

"I'm taking no chances," I tell them as I sit down at my station and start prepping for my first appointment. "In a few days, if he does nothing, I'll dial it back."

"Revenge doesn't have a timeline. Don't get too comfortable."

"Am I supposed to look over my shoulder forever?"

Pike shrugs. "Maybe, man. As long as he's out walking the streets, he'll always be a threat."

"Maybe he was just shit-talking. Maybe now that he's free, he'll drop whatever beef he has against me and move on with his life."

Gigi stands and stretches, pressing her fingers into her back. "Oh yeah. I'm sure he'll forget you and become an upstanding member of the community. He won't look at you like you stole his girl."

"I didn't steal his girl."

"Whatever you say, bud. The way he sees it and reality are probably two very different things. A man who thinks clearly doesn't put a tracking device in a person's car. Don't think rationally," she says. "You need to lean into the irrational."

"You think Stone has ever thought rationally?" Lily adds as she walks into the back to grab something out of a cabinet.

"I've always used my head."

"Oh please. The wrong one, maybe," Lily teases, riffling through the cabinet. "Got it." She pulls out a box, holding it up like we're about to clap, but no one does.

"I'm trying to do better…be better."

Lily ruffles my hair as she stalks by, heading to the piercing room. "And I'm proud of you, too."

"It's like you're growing up before our very eyes," Gigi teases me.

I lift both hands in the air, giving my middle fingers to everyone. I know they're joking, but it's at my expense.

"You're super touchy lately. You on the rag?" Pike asks, adding on to the bullshit from the women in the shop.

"Yeah, brother. I think we're in sync."

He laughs as he turns his back to me, going back to work. The day is only beginning, but I can already tell it's going to be a long one.

"Stone," Rebel calls from the front, "you have a visitor."

"Ooh," everyone in the back says, being assholes.

"I hate you all," I grumble under my breath as I climb to my feet.

I'm not expecting anyone to drop by today, and I run through a list of people it could possibly be. But the only person I didn't consider is standing in the waiting room with a smile on her face.

"Ma," I say, scrunching up my face like she's an illusion. "What are you doing here?"

She points to the door as Fran walks inside. "Giving this old bag a ride."

"Honey, you're not too far on my heels," Fran says back to her before turning her attention to me. "I wanted to take my girl to lunch and shopping."

"She can't go."

Ma rocks back at my words. "Excuse me?"

"Men," Fran mutters, rolling her eyes.

"I know Dad and Bear filled you in on everything that's happening. She needs to stay here."

Ma stands and makes her way toward me. "Says who?"

I touch my chest and pull my head back. "Me."

Ma tips her head back and laughs. "Your dad said the threat was against you and not Opal."

"Doesn't matter."

Fran cranes her neck toward the back. "Where is she, by the way?"

I pitch my thumb over my shoulder. "In the office, but she's working."

"Everyone needs to eat," Fran explains, like I've somehow missed a lesson on how to be human or a meal.

"I'm well aware of that, Auntie, but we just got here, and she needs to get some things done for Tamara."

Ma sighs. "He's probably right, Fran. We should let her get some work done. You know how swamped Tamara's been."

"Yeah," I say.

"Well, how about dinner?" Fran asks my ma.

"What time are you working until?" Ma asks me.

"Ten."

And here we go. There's their opening. I already know I fucked up as soon as the word left my mouth.

"We'll be back in a few hours to grab Opal. She can't sit here until ten," Ma says, "We'll bring her back here afterward if it'll make you happy."

None of this makes me happy. Not having a madman after me. Not having my mother and great-aunt take my girl out to dinner. Not having Opal in my presence at all times. It's all fucking miserable.

I rub the back of my neck, wondering how I can put an end to this. "It's not a good idea."

Ma touches my arm, giving me the same look she did when I was little and was fucking up. "You can't hover over her forever. We'd never let anything happen to her."

"I know," I grumble. "I trust you with my life." I don't want to tell her that I'm not sure if I trust her and Fran as a combo with Opal's. Fran has a way of being a distraction but means no harm. She's also usually the first one to stir the pot when things are going down. I swear she likes to see shit go haywire.

"We'll be back at six. No arguments," Ma says with a squeeze of my arm. "She'll come back to you in one piece."

I want to argue, but I keep my mouth shut. Opal loves my family, and it's only fair that everyone gets to know the amazing woman I can see in her. She has no one, and this is her chance to have everything, which includes me.

"Fine," I sigh.

The front door opens, and we all turn toward the rays of sunshine spilling through the opening. I see a large shadow, followed by my uncle's grouchy face.

"Bear?" I ask, shocked to see him here.

"Hey, kid," he says to me as he slides in next to his wife and places his arm around her shoulder.

She glances up at him, looking like her existence hangs on his every word. "Hey, handsome. Are you coming shopping with us?"

Bear shakes his head. "Working, babe."

"Damn. Where you headed?"

He looks right at me, and my blood boils. "Here."

"Here?" she asks, dropping her voice. "Why?"

"Bullshit," I mutter, reaching into my back pocket for my phone. "I'll take care of this."

"Make all the calls you want, son. I'm not going

anywhere," Bear says to me before giving Fran a kiss on the forehead. "I'll be home late tonight."

Uncle Thomas picks up on the second ring.

"Why's Bear here?"

"Hello to you too, kid," Thomas replies.

"Hello, Uncle Thomas. Can you explain why Bear is here?" I say as sarcastically as I possibly can.

"Because you can't look over your shoulder and tattoo."

"I hate when you make sense."

"He'll stay out of your way. You won't even know he's there."

"Unlikely." I stare at my uncle Bear as he stares back at me with a shit-eating grin.

"Just roll with it for a few days," Thomas tells me. "After that, we'll reevaluate."

"Oh my God. Hey," Opal says, walking into the waiting room behind me. "This is such a surprise."

Fran rushes away from Bear's side and moves straight to Opal. "Oh, honey. You're positively glowing."

"Anger has a way of doing that," Rebel mumbles, but no one else seems to hear except me.

"What are you guys doing here?" Opal asks, looking around at my ma, Fran, and Bear.

"I've got to go," I tell Thomas. "But we're not done talking."

"Whatever, kid," he says as he disconnects the call.

"Hi, Opal," Ma says, breezing by me. "We thought we could take you to dinner later. Would you like to join us?"

Opal glances at me as I growl.

"Knock it off," Ma warns. "You're not the boss of her."

Opal chuckles. "I love the women in this family."

"The men aren't half bad either," Bear says as he runs his fingers through his beard.

"I'd love to go to dinner with you two," Opal says.

Opal doesn't care that I'm bothered, which has me worried but also proud. She's coming out of her shell and doing it quicker than I thought possible. Being around all the strong women in my family is definitely rubbing off on her.

"Mama," Lily says in a sugary-sweet voice as she walks out of the piercing room. "What are you doing here?"

"Taking Opal to dinner," Ma answers.

Lily glances down at her fancy watch that tracks her steps and heart rate. "Oh. Early bird?"

Ma shakes her head. "No, silly. We're coming back later for her."

"Got it. And you." Lily turns her attention to Bear. "What are you doing here?"

"Protection," Bear states.

Lily tilts her head and nods. "Solid idea. I like it."

I roll my eyes with a huff. "Still bullshit."

"Think whatever you want, son. This is how it's going to be," Bear tells me.

Ma gives me a small smile, touching my arm again. "I know it's hard, Stone, but let someone else look after you for a bit. You can't protect everyone from everything all the time."

I grumble, but I'm not going to win. "I'll try, Ma. I'll try." She motions for me to tip my head and then kisses my cheek. "Thank you, baby. You made your old mom happy."

At least someone is happy.

20

OPAL

"This is lovely, isn't it?" Stone's mom, Mia, says as we sit at our table overlooking the Gulf of Mexico. "It's the perfect evening for this."

"The view never gets old," Fran says before taking a small sip from her ice-covered beer glass.

I stare out across the horizon at the endless blue of every shade. Since Stone took me to the beach, I've become obsessed with the way the water moves and sounds. I never knew something could be so calming while reigniting my soul.

"How did today go?" Mia asks, leaning back in her chair, one hand in the air with the stem of a glass of wine between her fingers.

She's a stunning woman with wavy, dark-brown hair and the most perfect, sun-kissed skin. At her age, I'd think she'd show more effects of aging, especially from the relentless and never-ending sunshine, but I'd be wrong because her skin is almost flawless.

"It was okay," I tell her, pushing aside my aggravation with Stone for making me stay at the shop all day. "I'm not doing it tomorrow, though."

Fran and Mia exchange glances, looking more than amused at my statement.

"Oh boy," Fran mutters against her glass. "This'll be fun."

"My son can be a bit much."

I nod enthusiastically. "A bit? That's an understatement."

"Like father, like son." Mia swirls her wine around in the glass. "They can be a pain, but it comes from a good place."

"That's the rub." Fran sighs. "They're being nice, but they don't know when they're overdoing things, or they think we're overreacting."

I reach out, dragging my fruity drink with no alcohol closer because I don't want to be dozing off after I get back to Inked. Drinking makes me ridiculously tired, and besides the chairs used for tattooing, there's nowhere for me to sleep off the effects. "I don't think Jeff's going to be an issue, and we're all changing our lives as if he's going to strike at any moment."

"Do you think people are inherently good?" Fran asks me.

I think about her question. Are people inherently good? I'd like to believe so, but my life experience has shown me

INFERNO

the opposite. There are more bad people in this world than virtuous ones.

"No. I learned that the hard way, Fran."

"Jeff's already shown his ass, honey. He'll think nothing of doing it again, and rarely do people back off when the fire's burning their feet. They run forward, right into a world of hurt."

She's talking in riddles, making my head hurt and making me regret my no-alcohol dinner.

"Maybe his time in jail changed him."

Fran tips her head back and cackles. "You're too precious, Opal. Too damn precious."

"Jail would change me," I mumble.

Mia gazes out across the water as her hair blows in the breeze. "Jail would change most people who think before acting, but let's face it, many men don't have that ability. They're almost feral."

"I'll drink to that," Fran says, holding up her glass for a second before taking a swig of her beer. "There's no almost about it, Mia. They are completely feral and sometimes unhinged."

"Why do we like them so much?" I ask them.

They have more experience with handling the other sex than I do. Lord knows I wasn't exactly skilled in my selection process before I met Stone. Even then, I didn't pick him as much as he picked me, or I fell into his lap.

"I didn't want to like Mike. God, he was so arrogant." Mia laughs.

Fran gives her an enthusiastic nod. "He was full of himself his entire life."

"The apple doesn't fall too far from the tree," I add, thinking about Stone's unwavering confidence. Instead of being annoyed by it, I've been drawn to his attitude.

"Stone's humble compared to his father. Mike was a world-class MMA fighter at the time."

I can see that about him. The man is a giant.

"How did you two meet?" I ask her, genuinely curious.

"He came into my ER after a match."

"Was it love at first sight?"

She shakes her head and laughs again. "I hated violence and thought his career was the worst thing ever. I wanted nothing to do with him."

"How'd that work out for you?" Fran teases her.

"The man is relentless." Mia shrugs both her shoulders with a hint of a smile. "Thank goodness for it, too. I would've missed out on a beautiful life."

"That's so sweet," I whisper, a little envious of the life she's led and hoping I can have the same.

"Two beautiful children, a husband who adores me, and a family that would move heaven and earth for me. I don't know what I did to get so lucky."

"You're a good person, Mia. Maybe one of the best of us. Although Opal's pretty damn sweet herself. She might give you a run for your money in that department."

"You think I'm sweet?" I ask Fran, my body a little warmer from her kind words.

"Baby—" she reaches out and places her cool hand over mine "—sugar has nothing on you."

I snort. "I do have a mean side."

Fran draws her hand away from mine and leans her body toward me, placing her elbow on the table. "What's the worst thing you've ever done?" she asks as she props her chin in the palm of her hand.

"Oh," I mutter, not having expected her to want details. What an idiot. Why did I have to open my big mouth? "I'd have to think about it."

Laughter bubbles out of Fran. "If you have to think about it, then I am right—you're nice to your core."

"We can't all be the perfect amount of sugar and spice as you, Fran," Mia tells her, joining in on the laughter.

Fran sobers. "There's no sugar in me, Mia."

I lift my hand, smiling. "I disagree. You've been nothing but kind to me."

Fran turns her gaze toward me with a soft smile. "You're special, kid."

"You pretend to be grouchy and sharp, but we all know the truth about you, Fran," Mia adds.

Fran's hands move to the table, and her fingers glide over her silverware. "Only to the people I love, and even then, it can get dicey at times."

"Got room for one more?"

I turn my head at the sound of the familiar voice as my heart starts to pound uncontrollably in my chest. "Stone, what are you doing here?"

"Baby," Mia says.

"We always have room for you," Fran tells him and motions for him to sit down.

"I was starving and couldn't pass up eating with my three favorite ladies."

I'm both happy and pissed. I'm happy he's here because I love being around him, but I'm also pissed because he couldn't let me out of his sight for a few hours.

The man doesn't seem to understand boundaries and the fact that I can take care of myself in many situations without needing a personal bodyguard.

"You missed us," Fran says, touching her chest with one hand. "We're flattered."

"Of course," he tells her, lying through his perfectly straight and white teeth as he makes himself comfortable in a chair next to me.

"Where's Bear?" Fran asks, craning her neck to look around the outdoor patio. "Did he come too?"

Stone shakes his head, blowing out a breath. "He got called back to ALFA for some emergency meeting, but he said he'd be back in a few hours. Figured it was my opportunity to dip out and enjoy a meal with the ladies in my life."

"That man loves his job." Fran smiles when she talks about her husband. Every damn time. She's so in love with him, and it's impossible not to notice. But it's entirely mutual.

"I had a cancelation," Stone adds, grabbing a menu that was left on a nearby table, "and had a few hours to kill."

"And you thought you'd come babysit?" I ask him, feeling a little spicier than normal.

"Oh boy," Mia mutters under her breath.

"Here we go," Fran says, leaning back in her chair and staring at us. "I'm here for this show."

"No show," I tell them, gazing right into Stone's eyes. "I want him to admit that he's here to watch over me because he doesn't think I can take care of myself."

Stone's jaw ticks, but his eyes hold mine without a single tell. "I know you can watch over yourself, Opal, but why would you want to when I can do it too?"

I turn in my chair, facing him head on. "You mean better, right?"

"Jesus," he mumbles. "You've been with Fran and Ma a little too much. They're wearing off on you."

"Is that a yes?" I challenge him, tilting my head and waiting for a response.

"Do we need to have another round like we did with the bat to prove who's right?"

"What?" Mia asks with her eyebrows drawn together and her eyes pinned on her son. "What about a bat?"

Stone shakes his head slowly and sighs. "It was nothing, Ma. We were doing some self-defense exercises."

"He had to prove a point." And while I may have lost the exercise, what happened afterward was worth the embarrassment.

"Well, did I prove it, or did you?" He smirks because he's thinking about that evening too. "If I remember right, we were both winners that night."

My face instantly heats. I don't need a mirror to know I'm blushing like a teenage girl.

"Ah, the food," Mia says, turning the attention away from us.

The waitress sets down three plates before her eyes land on Stone. Her entire body language changes as she soaks in his good looks and massive size.

"What would you like?" she asks him, but her voice is so husky, I'm sure she'd offer up herself as a meal if he asked.

"A salad. Whatever's quickest," he tells her, paying her no attention.

She doesn't scurry away. She's too busy ogling him to leave so soon. "Anything to drink?"

"Water is fine." He reaches out and places his hand on my arm, making it known we're together, together and dashing the waitress's dreams.

"She liked you," I tell him as I grab a fork with my free hand, keeping my voice low because Fran and Mia have started their own conversation.

"So do a lot of people, but there's only one person I care about."

"Stop," I tell him, feeling that same heat back in my cheeks.

He runs his thumb back and forth across my skin, staring at me. "You okay?"

I nod as I stuff my face with the most divine chopped salad. "Yep," I say, but it comes out all garbled because, of course, he has to ask me a question after the food's already in my mouth.

"Good." His shoulders visibly relax. "Are you sleeping at my place tonight, or are we sleeping at yours?"

I look at his aunt and mom out of the corner of my eye, hoping they're not paying attention to us. I don't know why it weirds me out, but it does. "It doesn't matter to me."

"My place, then. I have the better bed, and the two shower heads don't hurt either."

I can't argue with that. My place isn't shitty, but it's nowhere near as nice as his. He built his for his pleasure, whereas I was doing anything to survive, and finding an apartment on a budget and at the last minute didn't leave much room for fancy amenities.

"Maybe you two should stay with us," Mia says as she cuts her steak. "You'd be safer than on your own."

My stomach sinks. Not because I don't like Mia, but because I've already put enough people in danger. I don't want to add more to my list.

"We're safe at my place, Ma, and more comfortable, but we appreciate the offer," he answers, saving me from the awkward conversation.

"Can't have loud sex at the parents' house," Fran adds, plunging us right into embarrassing and awkward, almost giving me whiplash.

If I could crawl under the table and disappear, I would. But instead, I keep my eyes on my bowl, poking at the lettuce and jamming a big forkful into my mouth.

"Fran," Stone warns.

"What?" she answers innocently. "I'm only stating the obvious."

Ma rubs the back of her neck and says, "I'm not a fool, Fran. Stone's been having sex for longer than I'd like to admit, but I'm sure he could keep it in his pants for one day."

Fran snorts. "Did you forget what it's like to be in your twenties? It's on their mind every moment of the day."

"Some things don't change with age," Mia responds.

"Ma, please. Stop," Stone begs. "I like to pretend you and Pop never do that stuff."

It's Mia's turn to laugh. "Honey, how do you think you got here?"

"An accident the one time you did it."

"And Lily?"

"The other time."

Mia's laughter grows louder for a second, bubbling out of her. "You're precious and every bit your father's son."

"Can we stop the sex talk, please? I'm begging."

Mia nods at her son, but the smile hasn't left her face. "You know, if you're not careful, you could have an accident too."

"We've already discussed this. We're having at least four. Depends on when we get started." He's so casual with his answer and so sure of himself.

"Really?" Mia asks, but I can't read her face.

Oh boy. We had a one-time conversation about a possible future together, and he's already telling his family like it's set in stone. We've known each other such a short time, and the talk of a fairy-tale life was great at the time, but the chance of it becoming reality is still a toss-up.

A man who's never had a relationship can't easily become the poster child for monogamy. I've never seen it happen before, and I don't want to get my hopes up now that he'll become a changed man just because he met me.

It's all fanciful thinking. Dreaming is grand, but I won't allow myself to get lost in the idea of us becoming more. My heart's been through enough, and I'm already in too deep with him to come out of whatever this is unscathed if he were to walk away.

"I always wished I had more kids," Mia says. "But grandbabies are better. I get to skip all the bad parts and still have the baby cuddles."

"Damn right. Me too." Fran nods. "My feet swelled up like balloons, and I swear to God, my vag was never the same."

Mia snorts. "Kinda hard for it to be after a tiny human rips you open."

"Fuck," Stone groans, dropping his hand from my arm as he shakes his head. "I'm so happy I don't have my food right now."

"It's worth it, though," Mia says, ignoring Stone's complaining. "I have two beautiful children and grandchildren."

"At least the clit isn't harmed during childbirth. That would be catastrophic."

Stone throws up his hands. "Are you trying to chase me away? I mean, come on."

Fran cackles and Mia laughs.

I bite my lip, holding in my laughter. The big guy is uncomfortable, and the women are doing everything in their power to make sure he squirms.

"You're all wrong," he adds.

"It was supposed to be a girls' dinner, but you showed up. Now you have to deal with the consequences," Fran tells him. "Maybe you'll think twice next time, kid."

"There are other things to talk about."

"Periods?" she asks him with a raised eyebrow.

"Sweet Jesus," he mutters, holding his head in his hand. "They don't let up."

"You're too easy," Fran says, pointing at him with her fork. "Get a tougher skin. If you're going to have four babies, this table talk will be nothing compared to the things you'll see, hear, and experience."

"I can take it," he announces, puffing out his chest. "I'll deal with it all as it comes."

"Sure, big guy, sure," Fran says. "I hope I'm still around to see the day your first daughter gets her period. The meltdown…"

"From her or him?" Mia asks with a smile.

"Both," Fran answers.

And I know I want to be around for that day too, watching as the horror passes across his face and he squirms a little bit more.

21

STONE

The week has flown by, and Jeff hasn't shown his ugly mug. At this point, I am fairly certain he was talking the talk in jail to look like a dangerous man in front of the other prisoners.

"Now what?" Opal asks as we climb out of the truck at my grandparents' house. "I think we're safe."

"You can never be too sure." Even with looking over my shoulder constantly and keeping my eye on Opal, I've never had a week I enjoyed myself more.

Have I turned into one of them?

I busted my cousins' balls for years about being pussy-whipped and their need for monogamy, but here I am, experiencing the same thing and actually freaking liking it.

Am I old now? Does everyone hit this stage as they grow up?

I hate to think about myself getting older, but I am. The people my age are becoming fewer and fewer at the clubs I frequent in Tampa. That was the first sign, but I'd done my best to ignore it.

"I'm going to go home tonight," Opal says as she walks up the pathway to the house.

I follow behind her, snarling my lip at the thought. "We should talk about this." I can't keep the displeasure out of my voice. The thought of her going makes my stomach twist in a way I've never experienced before.

She peers over her shoulder when she makes it to the door. "I'm sure you'd like your place back. It's been fun, but don't you think it's time?"

I step in front of her, turning her face toward me with my fingertips. "Time for what?"

It isn't time for me to be alone again. I like our little fairy tale we've created this last week with each other, and the last thing I want is to pretend it didn't happen.

She stares up at me with round, doe-like eyes. "To go back to normal," she whispers.

I search her face, looking for something that says she doesn't really want what she's asking me for. She can't possibly mean what she's saying. "Is that what you want?"

She shrugs, tipping her head to the side.

I slide my hand back, cupping her cheek in my palm. "I don't want that," I tell her, brushing my thumb across her bottom lip. "I want you with me. Every night in my bed, every morning drinking coffee. But…" I pause, hating myself for saying the next words. "If that's what you want, I'll do my best to be okay with it."

"You'll do your best?"

"I'll be grumpy as hell for a little while."

A smile spreads across Opal's face. "You'd miss me."

"Something like that," I mumble.

Her hands find my arms, sliding up to my biceps and latching on. "Say it."

"Say what?"

Opal leans into me, pressing her breasts against my chest. "Say you'll miss me," she whispers, staring into my eyes, but it feels like she's digging into my soul.

I wrap my arms around her waist, holding her tighter against my chest. "I'd miss you, Opal." My voice doesn't even crack as I admit that to her.

She smiles up at me, making my insides all warm. "Was that so hard?"

"Not as hard as I thought it would be." I've never admitted my feelings easily to people, and with other women, I never even allowed myself to get close enough to form any. "But that's only because it's you, and I…"

"What?" she asks when I pause.

I lean my head forward, placing my forehead against hers, and close my eyes. "I think I'm falling for you and falling hard, and that scares the shit out of me."

"It scares me too," she whispers as we're cocooned together outside my grandparents' house. "I haven't felt this close to anyone in a long time."

"I've never felt this close to anyone else in my entire life."

I open my eyes and lock gazes with Opal.

"And then there's your family... God, I think I love them as much as you." Her eyes widen. "I didn't mean..."

I pull my head back, staring down at her beautiful face. "Do you love me, Opal?"

And for the first time in my life, I want her to say yes. I'm barely breathing, waiting for her to say the words. Maybe she made a mistake, using the term like she would if she were describing her favorite food.

She slides her hands to the front of my shoulders. "I do love you."

My heart almost skips a beat, and my stomach does this weird roller-coaster thing I've never felt before aside from being on a ride. "I love you too," I admit in a soft voice as the words feel completely foreign on my tongue.

"You don't think it's too soon to say it?"

"Are there rules to this shit?" I ask her, because while I'm experienced with women, feelings are an entirely different ball game.

She shrugs. "I don't know. I don't think so. It's not like I have a lot of people I can ask about this stuff."

"Then it's not too soon if we don't think it's too soon." I lean my head forward again, wanting nothing more than to kiss her lips.

But before I can, the front door swings open and Gigi, Tam, and Lily are standing there with goofy looks on their faces.

"It's about damn time," Lily says, clapping her hands.

"Fuck, that was painful to watch," Tamara adds with her arms folded in front of her.

"It was romantic," Gigi says, elbowing Tamara in the ribs. "Don't bust his chops now."

"What the fuck?" I snap at them.

"We were watching on the security camera. Sorry," Lily says with a pained smile, but I know she's not sorry in the slightest for what they did. "But it was also about damn time you admitted you were in love with her."

Opal laughs, not looking even slightly upset about my sister's and cousins' intrusion into our private talk. "See?" she says, ticking her chin in their direction, "I love them too."

The three girls come barreling out of the house, wrapping their arms around Opal and me. "We love you too," they say to her, squishing us with all their might.

"For fuck's sake," I grumble, stuck in an estrogen sandwich with way too many feelings. "You're all ridiculous and strange."

"Normal is boring," Tamara tells me, narrowing her eyes as she stares at me. "Get used to it, cousin."

"What's going on?" Gram asks as she steps out of the front door into the sunshine.

"They're in love," Lily says with her arms still wrapped around us.

"Anyone with two eyes and half a brain could see that, dear," Gram replies before turning back around and heading inside. "Don't let all the air conditioning out."

She isn't the least bit impressed by the revelation.

"Is she sick of our shit?" Tamara asks Gigi.

"Nah." Gigi shakes her head. "She loves us too much."

"Can we move this party inside?" I ask, starting to sweat from the heat of the sun and their bodies still wrapped around us.

Gigi peers up at me. "Can we hug again inside?"

"You're fucking batty," I tell her.

She gives me a wink. "Just fucking with you, but this was nice."

Tamara, Gigi, and Lily slowly unwrap their bodies from ours, and before I can finish the kiss I so badly wanted, Lily snags Opal by the arm and guides her inside.

"Fuck," I groan as I tip my head toward the cloudless sky.

"I'm proud of you," Gigi says.

I straighten my neck, looking over at her as she waits for me by the door. "For what?"

"I know it was a big step for you, but I don't think you could've picked a better person to say them to. You did good, little cousin. Don't fuck it up."

"I don't plan on it." I motion toward the house, wanting to get into the air conditioning. "I'm dying out here."

"This calls for a celebration," she says with her back to me as she walks through the foyer.

"Don't go overboard. It's not like I asked her to marry me. I said I love you."

"Pretty much the same."

"Hey," everyone says together, the news already spreading like wildfire.

I wouldn't be the least bit surprised if they had the

security footage up on the big screen, watching us over and over again. They're nosy enough to do that shit without any care for one's privacy.

I give them my usual chin lift, trying to pretend it's like any other Sunday.

"Love looks good on you," Fran says, letting me know that they most certainly all watched the security footage.

"Thanks," I say, hiding my annoyance the best I can.

"Son, come here," my pop says, motioning for me to haul ass in his direction with his index finger.

I mutter a slew of curse words under my breath because the guy can be such a sappy bastard. For his size and strength, my dad turns into a pile of mush whenever it has to do with love.

I take a few hesitant steps toward him, and as soon as I'm within arm's reach, he grabs my arm with his meaty hand and hauls me right into him. "I'm so proud of you," he says, almost suffocating me in a hug. "You're growing up."

"Don't get ahead of yourself, big guy," I mumble into his T-shirt, barely able to hear my own voice.

He pulls back, staring down at me with a goofy smile. "She's the one. I knew she was as soon as I saw the way you looked at her. Reminded me of myself with your mom. Apple doesn't fall too far from the tree."

I can't even argue with him. I was smitten with Opal the moment my eyes landed on her. I couldn't let Jeff treat her like trash. She deserved better—hell, everyone does.

"Can we not make a big deal about this?" I beg him, already more embarrassed than any other time in my life.

"Sure. Sure." He keeps smiling at me. "I just need one more moment to process this."

"Oh, for fuck's sake," I mutter, staring up at the ceiling while he gets whatever this shit is out of his system.

"You're such a big softy," Ma says as she places her hand on my father's shoulder. "Let the kid go. You're embarrassing him."

"Baby, he's not embarrassed."

"Yes, I am."

"Why?" Dad stares at me in disbelief. "There's nothing to be embarrassed about."

"It's not a big deal."

Dad puts a hand on each of my shoulders, lifting his head high. "Son, if you told every woman in your life you loved them, it wouldn't be a big deal. But besides the people in this family, you've never uttered those words to another soul. It's big. Really big."

"You're all going to freak Opal out and chase her away," I lie, wanting to escape from the lovefest with my parents and get back to my girl.

"Oh please. She knows we're weird, and she loves us for it," he says confidently, and he's probably right. "Although you're a handsome, smooth devil, I like to think we helped make falling in love with you so easy for her."

"It didn't hurt," Ma says, leaning against my father's side with her cheek against his shoulder.

"You can be a lovable bunch even when you're a little off," I tell them. "She may even love you more than me."

Dad scoffs with his head cocked to the side. "Nah. We made a good man, Mia," he says to my mom before turning his attention back to me. "I'm proud of the man you've become, son."

"Thanks, Pop," I say. "I learned everything from you."

"Okay. Okay. Enough of that shit. Get your ass over here and have a drink with me," Uncle Bear calls out from the other side of the room.

I look around, wanting for Opal to have a drink with us. "Where's Opal?"

Fran turns her head toward the door. "She ran out to get her purse."

"When?"

"A few minutes ago," Fran says before her eyebrows turn downward. "Too long ago."

I'm out of my father's grasp and hauling ass for the door before anyone else has a chance to move. My gut twists, and my thoughts turn to the absolute worst.

When I step out of the house, my truck door is open, and her purse is lying on the cement, contents spilled everywhere. "Opal!" I yell, knowing damn well she isn't here.

"I'll fucking kill him!" I scream, running toward my truck and taking off to find her.

22

OPAL

I'M NOT PAYING ATTENTION AS I WALK TO STONE'S TRUCK, drunk on the excitement of the day. Stone asked me to move in with him, and although there's a small part of my brain that doesn't want to believe he's as good as he really is, I've pushed aside the doubt and am following my heart.

I reach for my purse, smiling to myself.

I'm in love.

Not small love, but big love.

And for the first time in a very long time, I'm being loved back.

"Opal."

The sound of my name pulls me out of my love-induced haze. I spin around, expecting to see someone from Stone's family, but I'm met by a man I never wanted to see again.

"Jeff," I whisper. "What are you doing here?" There's a

slight quaver to my voice. I glance out of the corner of my eye, hoping someone will see him from inside the house.

"I came for you," Jeff says like it's not the most asinine thing in the world.

I blink, confused by the seriousness on his face. Not anger, but seriousness. He believes what he's saying, which sends my head into a tailspin. "You what?"

I stare at him, letting my eyes wander over his disheveled appearance. His T-shirt is stained, his jeans are covered in dirt, and his hair is greasy. He clearly hasn't been taking care of himself since he got out of jail because in all our time together, I never saw him like this.

"Let's go," he says in a stern voice.

"Go where?"

He reaches into his pocket, and I can't believe my eyes when he pulls out a gun. "Get in the car," he says, motioning with his head to the beater parked on the street. "I'm not asking."

Well, that escalated quickly.

I think about running, letting him chase me down. I know there are dozens of people inside that house who'll have my back, making sure he doesn't harm me.

But doing that will put them at risk.

They don't deserve it.

"You wouldn't shoot me," I say to him, trying to buy a little bit of time.

Jeff's face changes, and his seriousness turns into something more sinister. "I have nothing to lose."

I swallow down the fear that's climbing up my throat.

"Yes, you do."

He shakes his head with a smirk, waving the barrel of the gun in my direction. "I'll shoot you first, and then I'll move inside."

My insides seize at the thought of Stone's family being harmed. These people have been nothing but welcoming and loving to me. "You wouldn't."

"Are you willing to risk finding out?" Jeff raises an eyebrow.

I shake my head. I'd give my life before I'd let anyone in that house be hurt because of my dumb life choices and my poor taste in men. "No. I'll go," I tell him, glancing toward the house one more time.

I'm trying my best to use mind tricks to make someone notice I've been out here longer than I should've been. But I know how it is inside, and the likelihood is slim. Stone is tied up with his father, who's being overdramatic about our relationship.

I know I should stay.

I should stall.

Anything to keep him here and keep me safe.

But I can't do it.

I can't risk their lives.

I leave my purse dangling on the edge of the seat, sure it will fall out of the truck. A red flag for anyone, even a man like Stone. I move slowly, dragging my feet as much as I can.

But Jeff isn't having it. He grabs my arm, jerking me forward while pointing the gun at me with his other hand.

"Move it," he demands, all traces of the man I once had feelings for gone.

"I'm going," I snap as I grind my teeth together, wishing I were stronger or braver.

He pulls me toward the car, looking over his shoulder, past me to the house. He's waiting for them to come out. He's ready to shoot the first person who pops their head out the front door.

I move a little faster, not wanting anyone to get hurt. I don't hesitate in opening the car door and plopping myself down in the seat. "Let's go," I tell him as soon as my legs are inside the vehicle.

"I knew you'd come to your senses," he says, slamming the door, clearly out of his mind.

"What the fuck am I doing?" I whisper, toying with a piece of string hanging from the hem of my jean shorts. "He's going to kill me."

I inhale and exhale, each breath coming and going faster than the one before. My head starts to spin, and my vision blurs as I close my eyes, hoping to keep myself awake.

Do not pass out.

I can do this.

Do not pass out.

I can keep them safe.

I stare at the house as Jeff rounds the car. Every instinct in my body tells me to run, but I push it down, ignoring my inner voice. I can see the outlines of people through the windows, wishing I were in there too.

"Where are we going?" I ask Jeff as he gets into the car next to me.

The engine's still running. He knew this was an in-and-out deal, leaving the car on for a quick getaway.

"Where we can be alone. Far, far from here." He doesn't waste another second before he pulls out into the street, heading away from the house.

I breathe a sigh of relief, knowing they're safe.

My life has felt inconsequential for so long. No one really cared if I lived or died before I met Stone. I always felt like Jeff would rebound quickly if I disappeared, and I was spot-on. I missed the entire stalker aspect, but that has nothing to do with love.

"I've missed you," he says, staring at the pavement as he pulls onto the main road. "Life hasn't been the same without you."

"Okay," I mutter, not knowing what else to say.

"No one is going to treat you and love you as good as me."

I want to laugh, but I don't. Love isn't shown with force and definitely not with a gun.

"He doesn't deserve you."

That's a ridiculous statement. If anything, I'm the one who probably doesn't deserve Stone or his family.

I glance down at the gun Jeff has placed between his legs. The dumbass has the barrel pointed at his body.

"What happened to the blonde?"

His head snaps my way as we sit at the light. "What blonde?"

"The one you had at our apartment."

I lean over, debating grabbing for the gun.

Can I do it?

"She was nothing," he says, shifting in his seat as his gaze turns back to the road.

The real question is…should I do it?

I don't want to die.

Things in my life have been starting to get good for the first time in years. The last thing I want is to have it all end now.

I can get the gun from him, but I will have to be smart about it. I can't let him get me out of the car. I have to act fast before he takes me somewhere no one would ever find me again.

"If I can't have you, no one else can, Opal. You were meant to be with me forever."

Chills run down my spine as the reality of the situation crashes over me. I'm not getting out of this alive. I'm the only one who's going to be able to rescue me. No one's coming for me. Not because they won't try, but there's no time.

Jeff's going to use that gun on me unless I use it on him first.

There is no time to waste.

I lunge to my left, wrapping my fingers around the barrel, but Jeff's too fast. He slams his legs closed, making it impossible for me to pull the gun free.

"Fuck," he barks, yanking the steering wheel to the side and swerving through traffic.

I don't pull my hand back. It's better to risk dying in a traffic accident than to let him take me somewhere else.

I rear my free hand back and let it fly toward his face. My knuckles connect with the side of his jaw, and his head snaps back, sending the car to the side of the road. My ass lifts off the seat with a jolt, but I don't release my hold on the gun or stop hitting Jeff as he tries to fend me off.

Everything happens so fast, but somehow it feels like slow motion. I can hear the blood pumping through my ears as my heart hammers at a pace I don't know that I've ever experienced before.

I struggle to get hold of the gun, but Jeff's legs are too strong. He's doing his best to maintain control, and I know there's only one more thing to do.

I let go of the gun, sliding my hand out from between his thighs, and reach up. I yank the steering wheel as hard as I can before he has a chance to hit the brakes. When I look up, I see a telephone pole coming right at us.

I wince, closing my eyes, and let the impact happen.

It'll all be over soon…

My entire body moves forward as soon as the front of the car makes contact with the wooden pole. The airbag deploys, rocketing my body backward as it smashes into my face.

The horn is blaring, my ears are ringing, and my heart is pounding harder than it was only a few seconds ago. I'm dazed and confused, unable to focus.

People are surrounding the car, looking at us like we're a sideshow act.

"Don't move," someone says as soon as they open my door.

I open my mouth to say something, but nothing comes out. I want to warn them, tell them about Jeff and the gun, but I can't think straight or form any words.

"The police are on the way," someone says, but I'm not sure if it's the same person or someone else.

"Shit. How did they survive?" another person asks. "The car is crushed."

I let my head drift to the left where Jeff had been, but he's not there. Did he run away? How did he get out of the car so quickly? Is he outside, ready to shoot me as soon as he has a clear line of sight?

"Jeff," I mumble, his name barely audible.

"He's not breathing!" someone yells from the front of the car.

When I turn my head to look forward, my gaze lands on a giant hole in the windshield.

"Do I start CPR?" another person asks.

Everything is covered in a white haze, and that dull ringing in my ears continues, adding to the noise of the horn honking over and over again.

"He's dead," someone says.

He's dead.

Are they talking about Jeff, or did we hit someone in our struggle?

The white fog in my mind shifts, turning black, and then everything disappears.

23

STONE

I PLACE MY HAND ON OPAL'S SHOULDER, TRYING TO CALM her as she begins to stir. "Don't move. You're safe, baby."

"Thank goodness," Fran says, rising from her chair to stand on the other side of Opal's hospital bed. "I didn't think she was ever going to wake up."

Opal's face looks like she went three rounds in the ring with a heavyweight fighter. Her nose is swollen and packed with cotton. Her eyes are black, blue, and all shades of purple.

"Stone," Opal whispers, opening her eyes slowly.

"I'm here, Opal. You're safe," I repeat, wanting her to fully understand that she's not in harm's way.

She gazes up at me, but her eyes aren't focused. "Where am I?"

"You're in the hospital."

She tries to sit up and winces.

I push her down again as gently as I can. "Baby, you're

okay. Just a broken nose."

Tears form in the corners of her eyes. "Jeff?"

She looks so small and helpless in this bed. "He's dead. He went through the windshield and hit the pole."

She closes her eyes for a moment, letting those tears spill down her face. "I did it."

"Oh, honey. You didn't do anything but survive," Fran tells her as she grabs her hand and gives it a squeeze.

"No," Opal says, opening her eyes. "I grabbed the steering wheel. He's dead because of me. I crashed the car."

In this moment, I don't think I've ever been prouder of someone. I brush away the blood-caked hair from the side of her face. "You did good, Opal. You saved your life."

"But…" she starts to say.

I shake my head. "He killed himself. You didn't make him get in that car. He made you get in at gunpoint. If he weren't dead, I'd kill him myself."

"The man got exactly what he deserves, sweetheart. Don't feel bad about that. He would've killed you."

"I knew he would, and I couldn't let that happen," Opal admits. "I didn't have any other choice."

I smile down at her, hating that she's beating herself up for that asshole's death. "You're not in trouble. You did what you needed to survive. He got what was coming to him."

"I don't know," Opal mumbles.

"He never would've stopped, honey. Never. You would've had to look over your shoulder your entire life—

and Stone too. You never would've had peace. He brought this on himself. Wipe him from your mind. He isn't worth the time or the energy," Fran says to Opal.

"Knock, knock," Gigi says as she pokes her head into the room. "Can we come in?"

"A few at a time," I tell her, knowing damn well the entire family is in the hospital waiting room.

Gigi nods, motioning to someone in the hallway before the door pushes open and she, Tamara, and Lily walk in.

"Sweet Jesus," Tamara mutters, her eyes locking on Opal's black eyes.

"Those are some shiners," Lily adds.

"I have some concealer that'll cover those bad boys. No worries, babe," Gigi says, trying to keep the mood light.

Opal laughs, but her tears continue to fall. "You guys didn't have to come."

"Doll," Tamara says as she slides in next to Fran, "the whole family is here, and it's a requirement. When one of us is hurt, everyone shows up."

"Everyone's here?" Opal whispers, her eyes wide in amazement.

Lily nods at the foot of the bed. "Yep. It wasn't so hard because we were all together. As soon as we got the call from Stone when he found you at the scene, we hauled ass out of the house and headed here."

I'll never be able to get the image of Opal's motionless body out of my mind. Blood oozing from her nose, with her head tilted to the side. My heart stopped for a second until I could find her pulse, realizing she was knocked out and not dead. The ambulance arrived a few minutes later, but I stayed at her side, holding her hand until they forced me to let go.

"You found me?" Opal asks, her eyes soft as she looks up at me.

I lean over, placing a kiss on her forehead. "I'll always find you."

"Way to sound creepy, man," Tamara says with an eye roll.

"It was meant sweetly," Lily tells her.

"Thank you," Opal says to me, ignoring the girls arguing about my statement.

"Always, baby. I was petrified," I admit.

"I'm not as helpless as you think."

I shake my head. "I never thought you were helpless, Opal. I just want to be the one to protect you. I hate the idea of you being in danger."

"You can't protect me from everything and everyone."

"Obviously," I say, laughing a little, but hating that she had to go through all that. "You did good."

I feel like I need to keep repeating those words. She did the best she could and got herself out alive. Anyone would've done the same thing in her situation, but they might not have been lucky enough to survive.

"When you're all healed, we're going for drinks," Gigi tells Opal.

"Don't come in this week," Tamara says to her. "You need time to recuperate."

Opal shakes her head. "I don't want to take the week off. I'll be in tomorrow."

Tamara shakes her head. "Take two days, then. Boss's orders. I won't take no for an answer."

"Don't rush it," Lily adds. "You're still in shock, and tomorrow you're going to hurt like a mother."

The door to Opal's room opens again, but this time, it's my mom. "Girls, I want a moment," she says to Gigi, Lily, and Tamara.

"Yes, Ma," Lily says, touching the blanket over Opal's feet. "Rest up, sis. I'll come see you tomorrow."

Opal smiles, the tears streaming again. I get a little choked up myself, knowing Opal used to have no one, but now she has us. "Thanks, Lil."

"See you Wednesday," Tamara tells her.

"Call if you need anything," Gigi says.

The three girls peel away from the bed and head toward the door as my mother pushes it open farther and steps into the room. "Thanks, girls."

They nod in unison as they pass by her and disappear into the hallway.

"Opal," Ma says as she walks up to the bed, getting her first good look at Opal. "How are you feeling, hun?"

"Like someone smacked me in the face with a baseball bat."

Ma laughs, brushing back her long brown hair. "Looks like you were too."

"Ma," I warn, shaking my head. "Come on now."

Ma waves me off, ignoring me like she often does.

"Honey, she's going to see her face in a mirror, but thankfully, everything will heal. You got lucky."

Pop strolls into the room, holding a bag of garbage he grabbed from the vending machine near the waiting room. "Oh good. You're awake."

"Hi, Mr. G," Opal says to my dad.

"Look at you. A couple of shiners. Been there. Done that. Shit looks worse than it feels."

"Then mine must look god-awful because I feel like something's boring into my skull."

He reaches his hand into the bag, pulling out a couple chips. "It's the cotton they shove up there. It's the worst."

They're bonding over injuries. It's cute and ridiculous at the same time.

"We've been worried sick about you," Ma tells her, eyeing my father as he shoves the chips into his mouth like he hasn't eaten in days.

"You were?" Opal asks, her voice high and light.

"Of course," Fran adds, never leaving Opal's side.

"Kid, you're one of us now. When you disappeared—" Ma shakes her head and frowns "—I was scared I'd never see you again."

"She cried," Pop adds with a tip of his head toward Ma.

Ma raises her chin, glaring at my father. "Don't act like you were calm, Michael."

I snort. She's not too happy when she uses his full name. "We were all scared."

"I'm okay," Opal tells them.

Dad raises an eyebrow. "You sure?"

Opal nods and winces. "My neck hurts a little, and, of course, my face does too."

"You'll be sore for a bit. I could give you some exercises you can do to heal that neck faster."

Opal's grimace is unmissable. "I'm good."

The door opens again, and Uncle Thomas and Uncle James walk in, followed by a uniformed officer.

"I'm sorry to interrupt, Opal. The guy needs a statement," Uncle Thomas says, pitching his thumb over his shoulder to the guy who looks like he wouldn't know a smile if it hit him square in the face.

Opal lifts herself, shifting her body upright a little more. "It's okay."

"Ma'am," the officer says as he pulls a pen and a small pad from his black vest. "I'm sorry to bother you while you're recovering, but it's important that we get a statement from you as soon as possible."

Uncle Thomas looks at me and ticks his head to the side of the room with a window showing a view of the attached building's roof, where he and Uncle James are standing.

"I understand," Opal tells the officer.

I snarl, not wanting to leave Opal's side but knowing I have to give her some space to talk to the officer.

Opal gives my hand a squeeze. "It's okay, Stone."

I smile down at her before bending over, giving her head a light kiss. "I'll stay in the room."

"Thank you," she whispers, staring up at me in a way

that makes my chest tighten.

I stalk away from her and move to where Thomas and James are standing, and my parents join too. "What's up?" I ask them.

"She okay?" Uncle James asks, studying Opal as she talks to the officer.

I nod. "Banged-up, but otherwise, she's okay."

"And mentally?"

"She feels guilty," I tell him.

Uncle James tips his head and grimaces. "She shouldn't feel that way, but it's understandable. That feeling will wane once the gravity of what happened hits her. She did what she needed to do to survive, but she hasn't come to terms with that entirely. Watch her. Once she realizes how close to death she was, she may break down a little."

"Expect that to happen sooner rather than later," Uncle Thomas adds, moving his gaze to Opal. "She'll need you then."

"I don't plan on leaving her side," I assure them.

Ma grabs my arm, looping her elbow with mine. "I'm proud of you, baby."

I furrow my eyebrows, confused. "For what?"

Ma smiles at me like she did when I hit a game-winning home run in little league. "You're all grown up."

"Well, yeah."

"Mentally, baby, mentally. You must really love her."

"I do, Ma," I tell her.

"The reality of what happened is going to wash over

you too, Stone. Be prepared for that. Work through it fast so you can be there for her."

I nod. "I'll be fine."

"Said every man ever." Ma rolls her eyes. "Each one of you acts all big and tough, but you're all giant cinnamon rolls inside."

"Cinnamon rolls?" Pop asks, jerking his head back. "How the hell are we like cinnamon rolls?"

"You're all mushy and lovable on the inside," she explains.

"There're worse things to be called." Uncle Thomas shrugs.

"Like asshole," Uncle James says.

"I get that one a lot at home." Uncle Thomas laughs.

"Me too," Uncle James says.

"What's everyone talking about over here?" Aunt Fran asks, walking up to us and inserting her body in the middle of the group.

"The guys being asshole cinnamon rolls."

Fran's nod is immediate. "Perfect description."

"Is it going okay over there?" I ask Aunt Fran, glancing toward Opal.

My girl's looking at the cop, talking to him and not paying any attention to any of us. He's writing down everything she's saying, trying to keep up with her.

"Yep. She's a tough cookie. She's really been through some shit in life. It's about time she catches a damn break."

"I plan to make it happen," I promise.

24

OPAL

I place my hands on the countertop near the sink and lean forward, getting a closer look at my face. "What in the…" I turn my neck to the right and then to the left. "I look awful."

Stone walks in behind me and catches my eyes in the reflection in the mirror. "You look great." Somehow, he says those words with a straight face.

"Do you need glasses?"

He smiles as he wraps his arms around my sides, and he flattens his hands on my stomach. "No, baby. You're alive and breathing. Those eyes and that nose will heal. You're still beautiful to me."

I lean a little closer, which only makes everything worse. "People can't see me like this."

"If people stare, tell them they should see the other guy."

I roll my eyes. "That may work for you, but it's not as cute coming from me."

"Nah, it's badass." He bends his neck, placing his mouth on my neck.

I close my eyes, relishing the softness of his lips as I let my body lean against him. "How long is this going to take to heal?"

"A week or so," he murmurs against my skin.

"Damn," I mutter.

"The girls are going to stop by and bring makeup to cover it all… Is that okay?"

"Of course."

I'd never say no. I could have an eyeball hanging out of my head, and I'd say yes. I love being around them, along with the rest of the family.

He peppers my neck with light kisses, and I lose focus on my bruises and can see only him.

"You're too good to me," I tell him, placing my hands on his as they rest on my stomach.

"I have a surprise for you," he says, pulling his mouth away from my neck.

I instantly miss the heat of his body as he releases me. "What is it?"

He takes my hand and moves toward the door. "You have to see it. I worked on it while you were napping."

I've been out of the hospital for less than twelve hours. I can't imagine what it could be.

I follow Stone down the hallway to his spare bedroom.

He grabs the door handle and pauses. "Close your eyes first."

I do as I'm told, squeezing my eyes shut. I trust him completely. It may be the first time in almost a decade I don't doubt my safety in the presence of another person.

It's freeing.

The door creaks, and Stone leads me into the room.

My belly flips a little because I'm not used to surprises, especially not nice ones.

"Can I open my eyes now?" I ask after I stop shuffling my feet against the hardwood floor as he stops me somewhere in the room.

He sets his hands on my upper arms, giving me a small squeeze. "Open them," he whispers.

I open my eyes, soaking in what's changed. There's no longer a bed or the furniture that was in here before. Instead, I see a desk, a fancy chair, and a lamp.

"It's an office for you."

"For me?" I ask, shocked.

"You need your own space to do work or whatever. Do you like it?"

I turn around, and his thick arms engulf me. I tip my head back, peering up at him. "I love it. You're too good to me."

He touches his forehead to mine, gazing into my eyes. "You deserve it and more. I would've decorated it, but I want you to make it your own."

"Are you sure?"

He smiles, and my entire body warms. "One hundred percent."

"Can I paint the walls black?"

"Yes. If that's what you want."

"I want it. I want it badly." I give him a smile back. "I'm totally into moody paint."

"We will get your stuff in a few days and move it here."

"Okay," I breathe, loving the idea of moving in with him. "Are you sure this is what you want?"

He pulls his head back and furrows his eyebrows. "I'm fine with the black walls. Paint them hot pink if you want. It's your room to do with what you wish."

I shake my head. "I mean all of it."

"You want to paint the entire house black?"

I'd laugh if it weren't such a serious question I was trying to ask him. "I mean this." I lift my hands, waving them around, "Us. It's a big change for you. I kind of landed in your lap."

Stone's eyes flash, and his face changes. He reaches out, gently cupping my face in his giant hand as he gazes into my eyes. "Sure, it's a change to how I used to be, but I'm not that dumbass kid anymore. I'm a man, and when I see something I want, I go after it. I know what I want, and it's you, Opal. You may have walked into my shop without any idea of what was going to happen and how that night would change both our lives, but I wouldn't change a damn thing because it brought you and me here to this moment together. This was meant to be. I don't do anything I don't want to do, and I want you here. I want you with me. No more asking that question."

My stomach flutters at his words. I've heard them before, but today, I feel them. "Black, it is," I say, trying to break the seriousness of the moment.

"Are you sure you want this?" he asks me.

I snake my arms over his shoulders and around his neck. "I've never wanted anything more, Stone. I finally feel like I have a man who loves and cares for me and a family that thinks of me as one of their own."

"My family loves you."

I smile, knowing those words are the truth. "There's nowhere else I'd rather be."

"Because you want to be with me, or you want to be with them?"

"You, handsome," I tell him, toying with the hair near his neck, "but they're a bonus."

"Are you done questioning how I feel?"

I nod.

"I don't do shit unless I want to. I wouldn't be here if I didn't want to be here. I wouldn't be with you if I didn't want to be with you. You may have landed in my lap, but it's where you were always meant to be."

"Okay," I whisper.

"Okay." He smiles, pulling me in for a kiss.

I close my eyes as he presses his mouth to mine. I lean into him, letting my body relax against him, giving him all of my weight.

"Hello," Gigi calls from the front door.

"I hope they're not doing the naked tango," Lily says as Stone breaks our kiss.

He rolls his eyes. "She's so weird."

"I love her," I tell him, laughing at her use of words.

"What's wrong with you?" Tamara says, clearly talking to Lily. "Who calls it that?"

"I do," Lily replies.

"You sure you want to be part of this family?"

I nod. "More than anything."

"You're a weirdo too," Stone teases, pulling me out of the room with his arm slung around my shoulder.

If this is what it means to be weird, the last thing I want is to be normal. I've never felt so welcomed and loved as I do now.

"There she is," Gigi says as soon as we walk down the hallway.

Tamara jerks her head back when her gaze lands on me. "Holy fuck."

Lily elbows her in the side. "Way to play it cool, Tam."

Tamara glances down and rocks back on her heels. "I'm sorry, Opal."

"Don't be. I said the same thing when I looked in the mirror. I look worse than yesterday."

"It's part of the healing process," Lily tells Opal as she sets down a pink bag on the coffee table. "But we have everything you need to at least hide it."

"You don't want to scare small children," Tamara adds with a small snicker.

Lily turns an icy glare at her cousin. "Really?"

Tamara shrugs with a smirk. "Stop being so damn serious and touchy, Lil."

"It's okay," I tell Lily. "I don't think she's trying to be mean."

"She's mean naturally," Gigi says. "Bitch has always had a problem with verbal vomit."

Other people may take offense to Tamara, but I've been around this family enough to understand this is who they are and how they talk to one another. Nothing is done with malice.

"I have not," Tamara argues, plopping down on the couch.

"Babe," Gigi says and clears her throat, taking the seat next to Tamara. "I can name a half dozen times we almost ended up in a barroom brawl because of your big mouth."

Tamara touches her chest, looking far too innocent. "My mouth?" She laughs. "You aren't spewing puppies and sunshine out of your hole."

"I should've told them no," Stone whispers.

I slide my arm around his waist, resting my head against his bicep. "What fun would that be?"

"We could be doing the naked tango instead of listening to them bicker."

I giggle at his use of his sister's term. "There's always later."

He shakes his head. "Your body's been through enough. You need to give it time to heal."

"My body is fine. It's my face that isn't."

His green eyes move across my face, soaking in the horrific scene. "Your face is still beautiful."

I nod. "And it feels worse than it looks."

He winces. "No naked tango for you, then."

"Are you two talking about sex in front of us?" Gigi asks before she makes a gagging motion. "Stop it."

"You guys brought it up," he tells her.

Gigi instantly points to Lily. "She did. Not us."

Stone shrugs. "Whatever."

"I don't think we should put the makeup on her face today. It would be too painful," Tamara says as she pulls out a few bottles from the bag.

"I made an instruction sheet," Lily says, reaching her hand into the paper bag sitting on the coffee table.

"You mean a manual. It's five pages long and," Gigi says as she shakes her head, "has an accompanying how-to video tutorial."

"I wanted to make sure she knew how to use everything," Lily explains. She's totally cute, and I love her to pieces. She cares for everyone and is the sweetest of the bunch. It's not surprising since she's Stone's sister. They're not very different, although he'd never admit it.

"It's the best stuff they have. It's made to cover tattoos, so it'll cover those black eyes without a problem," Gigi tells me, holding up a tube of flesh-colored makeup. "I put in some samples of every shade."

"I don't know how to thank you," I say, giving Stone's side a squeeze.

"This is what we do. Better get used to it," Tamara says from her perch on the couch.

This is not what other people do. Although it's completely the Gallo way of being.

"But you can pay us back by going out for margaritas without the guys," Tamara adds. "Sometimes we need to talk without their nosy asses listening in on our conversations."

"Trust me when I say we don't always want to hear what you're talking about," Stone tells her. "The period talk can be a bit much at times."

Tamara laughs. "We only do that to make you uncomfortable."

"Mission accomplished," he mutters.

Lily walks over, holding the papers she so graciously wrote. "Ignore him. I know I do," she says about her brother as she hands me the instructions. "I've had a lifetime with him."

I hope to say those words someday too.

25

STONE

"Hey, kid," Uncle James says.

I rest my phone between my shoulder and cheek as I fold a towel. "What's up, Uncle?"

"I wanted to know if you and Opal can stop by the office later today."

I drop the clean towel into the basket and straighten. My stomach twists because Uncle James never asks me to come in unless there's some wild shit going down, and now here I am, going for the second time in a month. "Is something wrong?"

"Nothing bad. We found a few things that I think Opal needs to know about as soon as possible."

I turn my head, staring at Opal as she rests on the couch, still healing from the accident a few days ago. "Give us a couple of hours. Is that okay?"

"Sure thing, kid. I'll be here until five. I don't need you

two here for long, but I think this news is best delivered in person."

"You're scaring me."

"Don't be. It's only good news. I promise."

"She could use some good news."

"How's she doing?"

I blow out a breath. "She seems to be okay, but she's had a few nightmares."

"It's understandable. She went through a horrible and traumatizing ordeal. It'll take a while for her mind to catch up with reality. Give her time."

"I'll give her all the time in the world."

"I'm proud of you."

"For what?"

"Growing up."

"Whatever," I mutter.

"Seriously, Stone. This may be the first time I've seen you worry about someone other than yourself. The Stone of six months ago would've moved on already."

I rub the back of my neck, hating that he's right. "She's too good to walk away from."

"I felt that way about your aunt. I wasn't in a place in my life for a relationship, but I moved heaven and earth to make it happen. Hell, she didn't even like me very much, but I didn't let up. She finally came to her senses and knew I was the best thing to ever happen to her."

"You may be more full of bullshit than I am, Uncle."

James laughs. "Ask her yourself."

"I will. I'm sure she has an entirely different story than you do."

"I don't lie, kid."

I roll my eyes. "Yes, you do."

He laughs again, proving my point. "I'll see you later. A client just walked in."

"See you soon."

"Later," he says before disconnecting the call.

I jam my phone into my back pocket and walk into the living room to talk to Opal.

She looks up and immediately smiles. "You okay?"

"Yeah." I drop down onto the couch and pull her feet into my lap. "You up to getting out of the house for a bit today?"

She slinks down into the couch cushion, moaning as soon as I dig my fingers into the bottom of her foot. "I'm up for anything."

"You look like it," I tease her as she becomes one with the couch.

"What do you expect? You're rubbing my feet. Nothing else in the world matters right now."

"You're easy."

A smile spreads across her face as she closes her eyes. "I am not, but when you do that, I'll agree to just about anything."

"Anal?"

Her eyes fly open. "No," she snaps. "Put that in the no column for future reference."

"A guy's got to try."

"You shot your shot."

"And missed by a mile."

She laughs. "What did you really want to do today?"

"Anal," I tease her.

"Only if I can do it to you."

For a moment, I think if it's worth it. Would I let her do that to me in order to do it to her? It doesn't take me long to decide my answer is fuck no. I don't have many limits, but that's sure as hell one. "While your offer is mildly tempting, that's a hard no for me, babe."

Has a woman ever asked me to let her do that to me? I don't think so. If they did, I was clearly drunk enough not to remember the conversation.

"Scaredy-cat."

I move my hands to her other foot, giving it the same treatment. "Yeah, I suppose I am."

"Well, then what did you have in mind for today? I don't look the best."

I study her face, noticing the bruising looks worse than yesterday. The color is more prominent and has shifted. Bruises always get worse before they get better. The swelling in her nose has gone down, and she's been able to remove the stuffing. "My uncle James called and wants us to come to his office."

Opal leans up on her elbows but doesn't pull her foot away from me. Her eyes flash with panic for a minute. "What's wrong?"

"He said it's good news. Don't worry."

"No one calls you to their office for good news." She

pulls her foot out of my grasp and rights herself on the couch. "We have to go now."

"Now?" I stare up at her as she rises from the couch, looking totally panicked.

"Yeah. I can't wonder all day about what he has to say." She wiggles her fingers at me, wanting to help me from the couch. "Let's go, big boy."

Without hesitation, I take her hands. "I'm ready when you are."

She pulls me up with a groan, even though I didn't give her an ounce of my weight when I stood. "Give me ten minutes to fix my face."

I lift my hand to her cheek, cupping it in my palm. "Your face is perfect," I tell her, wishing I could carry her into bed and have my way with her.

"My face is a mess."

"Opal," I say, wanting her to hear my words. I know she hasn't had a lot of positive affirmation in her life over the last decade, but it's important for her to have that every day going forward. "I don't care about the bruises. You're still beautiful inside and out, baby. Don't ever doubt that. Do you hear me?"

She nods, not moving her face out of my palm. "I hear that."

"Do you believe it?"

She shrugs into my touch. "I don't know. I guess."

"We're going to work on that. Okay?"

She shifts her weight to her other foot. "Okay."

"Now, take that fine ass into the bathroom and throw

on a little of that shit my sister and cousins dropped off, and let's hit the road."

A smile returns to her face. "In a minute," she whispers.

"A minute?" I raise an eyebrow.

She nods as she rocks up on her toes, bringing her mouth close to mine. "I want a kiss first."

I bend my neck, taking her lips before she has a chance to take mine. I kiss her gently, worried about her nose and bruises, and wrap my arms around her back, wanting to hold her tightly.

She kisses me back, her body soft and warm, but her kiss firm and demanding. My girl's hungry. I've been treating her with kid gloves since the accident, too worried I'd hurt her.

When I pull back, she whispers, "I won't break, Stone."

She's giving me the green light, letting me know in her own way she wants more and is ready for it. "Now?" I ask, because I'm down to make love to my girl at every moment of the day.

"No," she murmurs against my lips. "We have to go, but later…"

"Later, what?" I ask, wanting to know if she has something planned in her mind. "Anal?"

She slaps my chest and pushes herself away. "You're an asshole."

"I want your asshole, baby," I tease with a smirk.

That statement earns me a middle finger as she stalks

toward the bathroom, leaving me in the living room with a boner and no reprieve.

"A guy can dream," I call out to her.

An hour later, we're walking into ALFA and holding hands.

"I'm nervous," Opal says, stopping outside the door to the offices to peer up at the sign. "Why am I so nervous?"

"It's okay. I promise."

If it's not, I'm going to kick my uncle's ass for lying to me. The last thing I want is for him to deliver news that will crush the spirit out of Opal. She's been slowly building herself back up, and knowing that Jeff will never be a problem again has helped, but she's felt a sense of guilt too, which I'll never fully understand.

"Uncle James wouldn't call us here without giving me some sort of warning if it was bad."

She turns her head toward me, her face paler than normal. "Are you sure?"

I nod. "I've known him my entire life. He's a good one."

Opal nods and takes a deep breath. "I'm ready."

I open the door and wait for her to go in first, following right behind her.

Aunt Angel's at the desk and rises to her feet as soon as we walk into the waiting room. "It's so good to see you two. Give me a hug," she says, outstretching her arms toward Opal and not me. "You're looking better. How are you feeling?"

Opal leans into the embrace and closes her eyes. "Better than I felt yesterday."

Aunt Angel pulls back, holding Opal by the shoulders to get a better look at her bruises. "Every day is a little easier."

"I'm having nightmares, though," Opal admits freely.

"You will for a while. I know I did when it happened to me."

Opal's eyes widen. "What happened to you?"

"I was kidnapped," Aunt Angel says so casually that if I didn't know any better, I'd think she was talking about the weather. "It was a long time ago, but the visions of what happened and the fear stayed with me for months."

"You were kidnapped?" Opal asks in disbelief.

Aunt Angel nods. "Yep. So was Izzy."

"No shit," Opal mutters, echoing my sentiment.

I thought I knew everything about my relatives, but clearly, there are large gaps in the information that has been left in the past.

"Suzy had a moment too where someone took her, but it was quick, though still traumatic as hell."

"What the hell happened in your generation?" I ask, wondering what shenanigans my aunts had been up to in order to get their asses taken.

Aunt Angel turns her eyes toward me. "Sweetie, if I remember right, your generation had their turn too. Gigi and Tamara are memorable off the top of my head."

I nod. "Damn."

We're like magnets for trouble.

"But it all worked out in the end," Aunt Angel adds. "Just like it did for Opal."

"Do you think about it a lot now?" Opal asks her.

Aunt Angel shakes her head. "I went to therapy, and the memory of that day faded over time. It'll fade for you. And there will come a time you will realize you haven't thought about it and it'll dawn on you, and you'll be shocked. But it'll happen. Life will go back to a new normal. It'll always be there. It'll be part of you, but it'll no longer be so in your face."

Opal touches Angel's arm. "That's good to know. Thank you."

I don't want Opal to relive the trauma of being taken by Jeff over and over again for the rest of her life.

"You're here," Uncle James says as he stalks down the long hallway between his office and the waiting room. "I'm glad you made it."

I give him a chin lift. "Of course."

He ticks his head toward his office. "Thomas is waiting for us."

"Both of you?" Opal says, her face suddenly pale again.

"We handle all family business together."

Angel smiles at Opal. "It'll be okay. I promise."

Opal nods and drops her hand from my aunt's arm. "I'm ready," she announces.

"Good girl," Aunt Angel whispers.

Opal slides her hand into my palm. "Stay with me."

I stare into her blue eyes. "I am never leaving your side, baby."

She smiles at me with her head slightly tilted down. She takes another deep breath and holds it for a few seconds before blowing it out. "Okay. Let's do this," she announces and walks toward James.

I follow behind, letting them lead the way. We pass by a half dozen closed doors. The office is quieter than usual, but it's later in the day. Everyone's either out on assignment or already clocked out, from my knowledge of how ALFA works.

"Bear here?" I ask Uncle James.

"He headed home after he finished his case a couple of hours ago."

"Cool," I mutter, but I'm a little sad not to run into him today. He always adds a sense of humor to any situation, even when it's uncalled-for and unnecessary.

Uncle Thomas is on his feet to give Opal a hug as soon as she walks in the room. "You okay, kid?"

Opal smiles as she wraps her arms around his body. "I'm great. How can I not be with such an amazing support system around me?"

I do have a kick-ass family. I was so damn lucky the day I was born to be dropped into an amazing group of people. I can't imagine what my life would've been like if I hadn't been.

"This is what families do for one another," he tells her, making it clear that not only do I think of Opal as one of us, so does everyone else.

"Take a seat," Uncle James says as I stand near the door being ignored while Uncle Thomas fawns over Opal, which I don't mind in the least.

"What's wrong?" Opal asks as she moves away from Thomas and pulls me toward the chairs on the other side of the desk.

Uncle James opens a red folder on top of his desk. "We did some digging after the shit went down with Jeff. Just in case there was any trouble, we wanted to be prepared to defend you. You never know how shit is going to swing anymore."

I wait for Opal to sit before I take the seat next to her. "We won't get into how fucked up that is and also somehow nice at the same time, but what did you find? We obviously wouldn't be here if there was nothing."

Uncle Thomas leans against a table off to the side, crossing his arms. "Opal, did you know your parents had a trust?"

"A what?" she asks, turning her head toward him when he says those words.

"A trust. It's similar to a will, but more rock solid."

Opal shakes her head. "No. I was young and had no one. After they passed, I ended up in foster care for a year, and then I was turned out with nothing."

Uncle James grimaces. "That's some heavy shit."

"It was probably better then that you didn't know and somehow got lost in the system, or your foster parents may have tried to fuck with the trust."

"Could they have done that?" I ask, totally clueless how the entire thing works.

"Anything's possible," Uncle James says, sliding the folder toward Opal. "Here's the trust paperwork."

Opal takes the folder off his desk and stares at the papers. "What does it mean?"

"It means you're a very wealthy woman," Uncle Thomas states. "It's fucked up that the person in charge of the trust didn't track you down, but thankfully, it seems like almost everything is intact."

I'm almost rocked back into my chair. *It means you're a very wealthy woman.* "No shit," I mumble under my breath.

For what feels like the first time, Opal's being given good news, and not only that, she's coming into a bit of money…something she's struggled with for so long.

"There's a bank account and some stocks. All of which have been transferred into your care. All the paperwork, including the power of attorney, is in the file, with your name as the trustee."

"Is there anything else?" Opal asks.

"There's a letter in there too. I had it sent overnight delivery because I knew you'd want to read it."

Opal pulls an envelope from the folder and stares down at it as she runs a finger over the faded ink. "It's my mother's handwriting."

My heart aches for her as she caresses the last remnants of something her mother left.

Opal tilts her head upward, and I see tears in her eyes.

"Thank you for this," she whispers, wiping her cheek where a drop has fallen.

"You're welcome," Uncle James tells her.

"There aren't any contingencies on the money. You can go to the bank as soon you'd like and transfer everything into your own account."

"How much?" Opal asks, still holding her mother's letter in her hand.

"After the sale of your childhood home right after they passed, the stocks, their savings, and the interest it's all accrued, it's well over half a million dollars."

Opal gasps as my stomach drops. "A half a million dollars?" she whispers. "Really?"

Uncle James nods. "A little more."

"Holy shit," I mumble under my breath.

"That's…that's…" Opal covers her mouth with her hand as more tears start to fall at a quicker pace. "I don't even know what to say."

"Say nothing," Uncle Thomas says to Opal. "We're happy we were able to find it for you."

"I don't know how I got so lucky," Opal says, looking around the room. "I don't know where I'd be without any of you."

"Better get used to it, baby. This is how we are. You're one of us now," I tell Opal, grabbing her free hand and lifting it to my mouth. "You'll never be alone again."

She cries a little harder, but somehow smiles at the same time. I give her hand a squeeze before releasing it again.

"If you run into any trouble, just give us a holler. We'll help in any way you need," Uncle James explains. "All of this may be a bit overwhelming."

"If the bank hassles you, don't hesitate to call. Someone will be there to have your back."

Opal straightens in her chair, still holding the envelope from her mother. "Thank you," she whispers.

"Thanks," I add, knowing words are not enough to express the gratitude I feel for putting a smile on my girl's face after the shitty time she's had since she was taken from my grandparents'.

"Now, fuck off. We have work to do," Uncle James announces, breaking the lovefest we were having in his office.

I'm the first to stand, followed by Opal.

"Are you okay?" I ask her as we walk out of the office.

"I couldn't be better," she says, tucking the red folder under her arm but keeping the envelope out.

"Are you going to read that?"

"Eventually. It's the last thing of hers. The last words I'll ever have from her. I don't know if I'm ready."

I pull her close to my side, walking in step. "You'll know when the time is right."

She leans into me, feeling more relaxed...almost lighter than when we walked in. "I don't think life can get better than this."

But I know she's wrong, and I'm about to prove it to her.

EPILOGUE

OPAL

The last six months have gone by in a blur.

My nightmares have subsided, only haunting me on days I'm overly tired. I do my best not to let that happen because reliving that day is far too taxing on me.

Stone has continued to be patient. He's the best thing that's ever happened to me. I never expected him to love me the way he does, but after watching how his father loves his mother, it's not the least bit surprising.

I'm still working for Tamara, loving having a partner to bounce ideas off when I worry I'm in a creative rut.

And then there's Stone's family. They've made me feel like I was always meant to be one of them. I don't feel awkward around them or like I don't belong. It's almost hard for me to remember what life was like before I met them. And that's saying something.

"Babe," Stone says. "What's wrong?"

I turn my head, staring at him blankly, lost in thought. "What?"

He brushes my hair over my shoulder as he studies my face. "I've said your name three times, and you didn't reply."

I shake away the cobwebs and memories. "I was thinking about this—" I wave my hand toward his family, who are spread out everywhere at his grandmother's house "—and how freaking lucky I am."

Stone's fingertips find my cheek, touching me ever so lightly. "I'm the lucky one."

I smile at him, wishing we could have more than a lifetime together. "I love you," I breathe.

"I love you too." Stone smiles, making my stomach flutter. I don't know how that's still possible after all this time, but it is.

"Well, aren't you two adorable," Aunt Fran says as she walks by carrying a tray of cannoli. "Giving me cavities from all the sweetness." She sends me a wink, letting me know she's happy for me.

"Stop, Auntie," Stone warns in a teasing tone to Aunt Fran as she passes us.

She's become a staple in my life. She's taken me under her wing and become something of a mother figure to me. She calls me every single day to check on me and find out how my life is going. That's something I've never had as an adult, and while other people may think it's annoying, I love it.

"You want to go for a walk?" he asks.

"You want to leave?"

I'm comfortable, and I look forward to Sunday dinner every week. Being surrounded by so many people, all of whom I love and love me too, it's more than I ever thought possible.

Stone laughs, shaking his head. "I need to stretch my legs a bit."

"Oh, okay," I say, but I'm not overly excited about leaving the comfort of the air conditioning.

The sun is exceptionally strong today, and the humidity is off the charts. The thought of walking into the extreme heat makes me sweat before I even step outside.

"We'll be back before they break out dessert," he promises, climbing to his feet.

When he holds out his hands, I take them, knowing I'm going wherever he does. "I don't want to miss a cannoli."

"Are they your favorite?"

"Only the ones with the ends dipped in chocolate."

Stone stops near the dining room, where Fran is placing the tray of cannoli on the table. "Fran, save Opal a chocolate one, 'kay?"

She nods. "You got it. You guys going somewhere?"

"A walk," Stone says as I slide my sunglasses over my eyes, readying myself for the brightness.

They exchange a look, one I can't place, even though I thought I'd learned all their looks by now.

"Take your time. Your cannoli is safe with me," she tells him.

"Thanks, Aunt Fran," I tell her, walking as slowly as I possibly can as Stone drags me toward the door.

"We're only walking down to the Gulf and back. Anything longer and we'd melt."

"I may melt before then," I tell him as I'm blasted by the heat as soon as he opens the door.

"Damn," he mutters, stepping into the sun and looking every bit like a Greek god. "It's awful out here."

"You want to skip it?" I'm hoping like hell that he says yes, but he kills all that when he shakes his head.

"We'll be back in fifteen."

Fifteen minutes is a long time to walk around in the recesses of hell. That's what Florida feels like in the middle of summer. Everyone thinks June is bad, but they haven't met mid-August.

"We should jog."

He turns his head, looking at me like I have three heads. "You want to jog?"

I shrug. "It'll go faster."

"But you hate exercise."

"I hate melting into the cement more."

"Want to race?"

"Uh, no," I laugh, pulling back on his hand so he doesn't get any thoughts to act on his idea. "I don't want to take a trip to the ER today."

Thankfully, the water isn't too far from the house. The closer we get, the stronger the breeze. It's the only saving grace of the walk.

"It's always so beautiful." I stare out over the turquoise

water, remembering the first time Stone took me to the beach. "I could look at it for a lifetime and never get sick of it."

When I turn to look at Stone, he's down on one knee.

"What are you doing?" My heart races, and I'm on the verge of throwing up from excitement.

"Opal," he says and pauses, thrusting his hand upward with the biggest diamond ring I've ever seen in my entire life. "I've never been as happy as I've been since the day you walked into my life. We haven't known each other long, but I know exactly what I want…who I want forever."

"Yes," I say before he has a chance to ask me the big question. I throw myself into his arms.

Stone tumbles backward, and I fall on top of him. He laughs, wrapping his arms around me. "I didn't get to ask the question."

I stare down at his handsome face so filled with love and life. "Ask me."

He lifts his head, taking my lips with his. "Opal, will you marry me?" he murmurs against my lips.

"Yes. Yes. Yes," I say against his mouth, hoping our lives are always this happy, but maybe not always this hot.

THANK YOU FOR READING INFERNO. There's only one more book left in the Men of Inked Heatwave series. **CINDER** is now available for preorder on all retailers and it's going to be a wild, steamy ride. Want a sneak peek of CINDER? *Turn the page to read the first chapter now.*

There's still one last scene between Opal and Stone. When I finished writing this book, I knew it was missing something. So, if you want to be a guest at their wedding and watch as Opal officially becomes a member of the family, CLICK HERE.

CINDER - CHAPTER 1
ASHER

"Bless your heart," my gram says to the cashier as she counts the change wrong for the third time. "Keep the change, honey."

"Are you sure, Mrs. Washington?" The cute girl looks dumbfounded.

"Yes, child. I'm sure," Gram says, smiling sweetly—although she's anything but, especially when people aren't bright.

I grab the bags, heading toward the door with my gram at my side.

"The girl's lucky she was born with beauty. She sure didn't get an ounce of brains," Gram says, hoisting her purse strap onto her shoulder.

"That's not very nice, Gram."

"I said she was beautiful."

"And dumb," I remind her.

She shrugs as we walk toward my truck. "We can't all

have everything, baby. But I'm telling you right now, always go for brains first and beauty second. Looks change. Smarts don't."

"Asher? Asher Gallo?" a female voice calls out, making me turn my head.

"Sweet baby Jesus," my gram mutters. "Here we go."

That's when I see her. A girl I haven't seen in a handful of years, and the last time I laid eyes on her, she was nowhere near as stunning as she is now. "Asher. Oh my God. Asher. Look at you," she says, rushing up to me and throwing her arms around me.

"Olive?" I whisper, unable to stop myself from hugging her back even with my hands full of groceries.

I knew Olive Thornberry for the first sixteen years of my life, but then her family moved away, and I hadn't seen or talked to her since.

"I've missed you," she breathes into my ear, sending goose bumps scattering across my skin even under the sweltering rays of the sun.

"You too, Olive," I say to her, pulling away to get a better look at her face but regretting the loss of contact at the same time. "What are you doing in town?"

"I've been staying at my grandparents while they're on a cruise to checked out the USF campus for grad school, but I'm heading back out tomorrow," she blurts out, barely taking a breath.

"Grad school?"

She nods, beaming with so much pride. "I got accepted into a medical research program there and start this fall."

"A smart one," Gram says, elbowing me in the ribs. "Beauty too."

I ignore my grandmother and keep my focus on the beautiful brunette in front of me. "That's impressive."

Olive shrugs like it's no big deal, but it very much is. "It'll only be impressive if I can finish the program. Getting in isn't the hardest part."

"I'm sure you'll kill it."

"Enough about me. How are you?" she asks, her eyes roaming away from my face. "You look…" she smiles softly, soaking me in "…well."

"Kids today," Gram whispers under her breath from behind me. "Asher, mind if I wait in the car while you two catch up? It's too hot out here for an old woman such as myself."

I look back and down at my short little grandmother, wiping the sweat from her brow. "Sorry, Gram. Let me get the door for you."

I pull the key fob from my pocket, starting the truck and unlocking the door. "Give me a minute," I tell Olive before helping my gram.

Gram leans over as soon as she takes my arm. "Invite her to the party."

"What?" I ask, shocked because my gram doesn't like any woman I'm even remotely interested in, and most certainly doesn't ask for them to come by when we're about to have a family celebration. "Are you serious?"

She peers up at me, staring into my eyes with so much seriousness. "Do I ever joke?"

CINDER - CHAPTER 1

She has a point. The woman is as serious as they come and has only grown more serious with age. "Not really. You say it straight, Gram."

"Ask Kalamata over for dinner."

"Olive, Gram."

"That's what I said," she tells me like she's in the right, when she very much isn't. "Ask her over. Do not let that one walk away without setting, at the very least, a date."

"I don't think—"

"You never think when it comes to women, child. Maybe for once, you should. Listen to me when I tell you, do not let her walk away. I see the way she looks at you and the way you look at her. That doesn't happen every day."

"What look?"

"Men are clueless beasts," she says to herself as she climbs up into my pickup truck, holding the grab bar and sliding in like she's done it a million times. "Now, go. I don't have all day. We have food to finish."

I set the groceries in the back before leaving my gram in the air-conditioned truck. I don't need to turn around to know she's watching us, judging my every movement, and probably having an entire conversation with herself about what a dumbass walking hormone I am at this point.

Olive's exactly where I left her, fiddling with the hem of her flowery sundress and staring at me. She's no longer the awkward teenager with braces and long, skinny arms. "Your gram seems nice."

"Seems is the operative word."

Olive laughs, and the sound is utterly beautiful. "I'm sure she's not that bad."

"She is. Trust me. She's the devil in disguise."

"I think all older women are," she says, touching my arm and instantly sending shock waves through my system.

I ignore the sensation, knowing my dick has a mind of its own. "If you're not doing anything today, you can find out for yourself. We're having a casual party at her house in a few hours, but no pressure."

"I'm sure she has enough mouths to feed without adding another."

"Don't be silly. She insisted that I ask you."

Olive turns her green-eyed gaze toward my truck. "She wants me to come?"

"She does."

She blinks, looking shocked. "Why?"

"A pretty girl with brains. Killer combination."

Olive laughs again. "We're not uncommon, Asher."

I tuck my hands into my pockets, knowing exactly what kind of women I have been hanging out with, and it's not the brainiacs. "Never said you were, Oli. Anyway, I'd love to catch up and hear about school and your family. Maybe think about dropping by, and you can watch the devil in action."

She holds out her hand. "Give me your phone."

I don't even hesitate to pull it from my back pocket, unlocking it, and hand it over to her. Spending the evening talking to Olive will be better than anything else I'd do for the evening. I've heard every story, listened to the same complaining about the exact same topics over and over again. It's mind-numbing.

Her phone dings in her back pocket. "I have your number, and now, you have mine. Text me the address, and I'll drop by later. What can I bring?"

"Can you cook?"

"Asher Gallo. I'm a good Southern girl. Of course I can cook, and I do it well."

The girl is getting more and more perfect, and maybe it's seeing her after so many years, but now I wonder why we never dated. "Bring anything you want. Whatever you have time for, or just bring yourself. We always have tons of food. Too much, really."

"Hush it. There's no such thing as too much food."

"I hope you like to eat, then."

"I do."

"Asher, time's slipping!" Gram yells from the truck before slamming her door.

"The devil calls," I say to Olive. "See you later, then?"

"I wouldn't miss it for the world," she tells me, and for the first time in years, I'm excited about the possibilities.

Are you ready for Asher's story? Preorder your copy of **CINDER** by tapping here.
Don't miss the final book in the Men of Inked Heatwave series!

Have you read the Original Men of Inked series?

Join Joe, Mike, Izzy, Thomas, and Anthony as they search for their true love and a happily ever after.

SEE WHERE YOUR FAVORITE SERIES STARTED!

Please visit *menofinked.com/inked-series* to learn more and start your next favorite read!

OPEN ROAD SERIES

Book 1 - Broken Sparrow (Morris)
Book 2 - Broken Dove (Leo)
Book 3 - Broken Wings (Crow)

BE A GALLO GIRL...

Want to be the first to hear about the next Men of Inked book or everything Chelle Bliss? Join my newsletter by [tapping here to sign up](#) or visit *menofinked.com/inked-news*

Want a place to talk romance books, meet other bookworms, and all things Men of Inked? Join Chelle Bliss Books on Facebook to get sneak peeks, exclusive news, and special giveaways.

ABOUT THE AUTHOR

I'm a full-time writer, time-waster extraordinaire, social media addict, coffee fiend, and ex-history teacher. *To learn more about my books, please visit menofinked.com.*

Want to stay up-to-date on the newest
Men of Inked release and more?
Join my newsletter at *menofinked.com/news*

Join over 10,000 readers on Facebook in Chelle Bliss Books private reader group and talk books and all things reading. Come be part of the family!

See the Gallo Family Tree

Where to Follow Me:

- facebook.com/authorchellebliss1
- instagram.com/authorchellebliss
- bookbub.com/authors/chelle-bliss
- goodreads.com/chellebliss
- tiktok.com/@chelleblissauthor
- amazon.com/author/chellebliss
- twitter.com/ChelleBliss1
- pinterest.com/chellebliss10

Made in United States
Orlando, FL
11 June 2023